That was a... have happe... herself, knowing that she should never have let it take place! To allow her boss to kiss her, really kiss her, in an unbelievably heart-stopping way, was pure madness! Their relationship...association—whatever the word was—was going somewhere neither of them wanted!

Well, she was sure *he* didn't want it, and *she* couldn't afford to want it! They could never have a business arrangement now, after that, surely!

Susanne James has enjoyed creative writing since childhood, completing her first—sadly unpublished—novel by the age of twelve. She has three grown-up children who were, and are, her pride and joy, and who all live happily in Oxfordshire with their families. She was always happy to put the needs of her family before her ambition to write seriously, although along the way some published articles for magazines and newspapers helped to keep the dream alive!

Susanne's big regret is that her beloved husband is no longer here to share the pleasure of her recent success. She now shares her life with Toffee, her young Cavalier King Charles spaniel, who decides when it's time to get up (early) and when a walk in the park is overdue!

Recent titles by the same author:

THE MASTER OF HIGHBRIDGE MANOR
THE BOSELLI BRIDE
THE PLAYBOY OF PENGARROTH HALL

BUTTONED-UP SECRETARY, BRITISH BOSS

BY
SUSANNE JAMES

First published in Great Britain 2010
Harlequin Mills & Boon Limited,
Eton House, 18-24 Paradise Road, Richmond, Surrey TW9 1SR

© Susanne James 2010

ISBN: 978 0 263 87870 7

Harlequin Mills & Boon policy is to use papers that are natural, renewable and recyclable products and made from wood grown in sustainable forests. The logging and manufacturing process conform to the legal environmental regulations of the country of origin.

Printed and bound in Spain
by Litografia Rosés, S.A., Barcelona

BUTTONED-UP
SECRETARY,
BRITISH BOSS

CHAPTER ONE

SABRINA'S heartrate quickened slightly as she walked along the unfamiliar street. If it wasn't for the money that was being offered for this post, no way would she have considered applying for it, she assured herself. But the straitened circumstances they were in at the moment left her little option. She would have to bite the bullet and hope that her face fitted.

Most of the houses in this part of north London were rather grand, Sabrina noted, yet now and again a distinct shabbiness was apparent. But when she arrived at the one she was looking for—number thirteen—she saw at once that it stood out from the others. And why wouldn't it, when you considered who lived there? The imposing, deep-blue front door had been freshly painted, its brass knocker and bell-push gleaming brightly in the mid-morning September sunshine.

She pressed the bell once—its discreet tone reminding her of the one at the dentist's—and waited, trying to imagine what her interviewer, the world-renowned author, might look like in the flesh. Of course, she'd seen him featured in the newspapers from time to time, but press photographs were never accurate or flattering.

Suddenly, the door was opened by the man himself— and Sabrina recognized him straight away. He must be nearing forty by now, she thought instinctively. His dark, tousled hair had begun to grey slightly at the temples, and there were discernible frown lines on the handsome, rugged face. But the penetrating, inky blue-black eyes were clear and discerning as he looked down at her. His expression was somewhat implacable, though not unfriendly, as he opened the door wider.

'Ah, good—Sabrina Gold?' When Sabrina smiled up at him in acknowledgement, he said, 'I'm Alexander McDonald. Come in. You found us all right…clearly,' he added.

His voice was businesslike, strong and authoritatively resonant, and Sabrina couldn't help feeling just slightly in awe of him as he led her up the thickly carpeted stairs to the first floor of his house. Treading carefully behind, Sabrina was more than aware of his athletic, vigorous body. He obviously worked out daily, she thought, no doubt with a personal trainer. Well, he and his equally famous brother Bruno—the well-known impresario with so many successful musicals to his credit—seemed to hold a permanent position in the Times Rich List. They could have whatever they wanted of this world's goods.

Realizing that she'd barely spoken since her arrival, Sabrina cleared her throat. 'Actually, I don't know this part of the city,' she said. 'But I had no problem finding you. And the walk from the tube was quite pleasant, especially in this sunshine.'

He glanced back at her casually as she spoke, feeling reasonably cheered at his first impression of her. She was simply dressed in jeans and a cream shirt, her long, fair hair pulled well back from a somewhat nondescript face which was devoid of any make-up, he noted. But she had expressive, large, grey-green eyes which he found interesting; they had a most unusual, feline shape.

They reached the first floor and he pushed open a door at the top, ushering Sabrina in before him, and as she brushed past he caught the drift of the perfume she was wearing, only just enough for him to be aware of it. Good; women who soaked themselves in heavy scents unnerved him. It was something he'd always hated. Since of necessity the successful applicant for the vacant post of his personal assistant would be sharing his space for a good part of every day over the next few months, it was essential that he found her presence acceptable. If ever she was going to materialize, he thought ruefully. Was Miss Gold number six or number seven so far? he thought wearily. He'd lost count.

Sabrina took in her surroundings at a glance. It was a large, high-ceilinged room, its full-length windows permitting daylight to reach every corner. A huge Persian rug covered much of the well-worn dark-oak flooring, and generously stocked bookshelves lined the walls. The whole room was dominated by an untidy, massive mahogany desk holding a computer and telephone and littered with random sheets of paper and other writing materials. Slightly apart from it was another, smaller desk with another computer—obviously awaiting Alexander McDonald's new assistant, Sabrina thought. There were also a couple of easy chairs and at the back, away from the light, was a *chaise longue* covered in brown velvet with a few cushions scattered on it haphazardly.

Alexander pushed one of the easy chairs forward. 'Have a seat, um, Miss Gold,' he said, as if he'd already forgotten her name, before moving behind the desk and seating himself in his large leather-upholstered swivel chair.

Doing as she was asked, Sabrina looked across at him steadily, trying to remind herself that she was here for one reason only—to secure the very highly paid employment he was offering, which could be hers if luck was on her side.

He came straight to the point. 'I see you have a degree in psychology,' he said, glancing down at some papers on his desk. 'Are you sure that this job, working for me, is what you want? What you think you can…tolerate, shall we say?' he added, the uncompromising mouth twisting slightly at one corner. The remark surprised Sabrina. She hadn't anticipated any degree of diffidence from Alexander McDonald. She decided she wasn't going to tip-toe around—she'd tell him the truth and be done with it.

'I think what you really want to know, Mr McDonald, is why I am not using my qualification,' she said coolly. 'And the answer is that it is difficult, with all the cut-backs, to get suitable work in my own field at the moment. My department was halved last year, and I was one of the unlucky ones that had to be let go. I'm sure you've heard the term.' She paused. 'It means that I was sacked for being too highly qualified and they could no longer afford to pay me on that level—and I was not prepared to accept the rather demeaning position I was offered instead.'

She hesitated before adding, 'The salary which the agency told me you were prepared to pay the right person encouraged me to try and persuade you that I could be the one.' She swallowed, realizing how awful that must sound, avaricious and money-grabbing. She might as well explain now, she thought desperately. 'It isn't that I *want* the money,' she said quietly. 'I need the money. And I've decided that I have to aim high.' If only he knew, she thought. They had just acquired their first house—their first real home after always living in rented places—and with it a rather crippling mortgage.

He paused for a moment before speaking, his observant eyes noting the rosy flush which had swept her cheeks, and his heart warmed instinctively at her words. He liked honesty in a woman—in anyone—and she had just been childishly direct. She could have made any other excuse for wanting to try something different. He looked down at the papers again.

'I see that you have all the necessary business skills, and are more than computer literate,' he said. 'Which is an essential requirement, because computers and I are often not best friends.' He looked up at her again briefly. 'A note pad and pen are usually sufficient for my own needs but unfortunately my agent, and my editor, both require something more technical from me—and, I suppose, something more legible,' he added.

Sensing that the interview was going quite well, Sabrina said calmly, 'I am well acquainted with most office machinery, Mr McDonald, but of course I would like some idea of what else the job might entail.'

There was silence for a few moments while Sabrina studied the carpet beneath her feet as she waited for him to answer her.

'Are you married, Miss Gold?' he asked bluntly, looking across at her again. 'Have you family? Children?'

'I am not married,' Sabrina answered. 'I live with my sister.' She paused. 'It's just the two of us,' she added. 'And last year I decided—I mean, *we* decided—to buy our own house, which I am desperate not to lose.'

He nodded. 'Does your sister work?' he asked.

Sabrina looked away for a second. 'Um, well, not all the time,' she said carefully. 'She has always been somewhat fragile, and succumbs to minor things now and again which tend to set her back. When she's well enough, she runs aerobics classes, and teaches dance and keep-fit very successfully.' She swallowed. She was not going to tell him that Melly was a brilliant dancer, and fabulous singer, and that she'd auditioned twice for his brother but had never been successful, had never managed to hit the big time in the theatrical world.

Alexander had been watching her as she'd spoken, watching the fleeting expressions which mirrored her thoughts. He sat forward suddenly, picking up a pen and twirling it between his finger and thumb.

'What I'm actually looking for, Miss Gold, is a PA,' he said. 'And I have to say that the hours are not necessarily nine to five. If there's a deadline I'm having difficulty with, I'd expect you to stay late sometimes. You know what I do; I write books on all kinds of subjects.' He leaned back, running a hand through his hair. 'My last assistant, who'd been with me for many years, finally admitted defeat and retired.'

He looked up at the ceiling for a moment. 'She now spends all her time in her garden, where she keeps some chickens—a lifelong ambition of hers, apparently.' He shook his head slightly, as if marvelling at the vagaries of human nature. 'Anyway, my filing system is wrecked and I need a reader, an editor, someone strong enough to cope with me when I'm frustrated. I need someone to type up my work when I don't feel like doing it, someone to field almost all my telephone calls and to be able to find all the things I keep losing.' He paused. 'I'm afraid I'm somewhat a nightmare to be around at times. Do you—do you think you're capable of meeting all those requirements?'

Sabrina let his words float into the air for a few

moments before a slow smile spread across her features. In spite of herself, she was beginning to like Alexander McDonald.

'Mr McDonald,' she said in the gentle tone she had often used when dealing with disturbed clients, 'I think you could safely leave everything to me.'

Putting his pen down, he stood up immediately and came around the desk, holding out his hand. 'Then it's a done deal,' he said, looking down at her solemnly. 'Can you start next week?'

Sabrina automatically slowed her steps as she walked up the short path of their modest semi-detached house on the outskirts of the city, admitting to feeling both elated and disturbed by her encounter with Alexander McDonald. He was undeniably drop-dead gorgeous, she thought. Did she really want to be working so closely with someone like him? Did she dare risk it, dare risk her feelings being churned up all over again? Because she was honest enough to realize that it was a distinct possibility—something she could well do without.

As she went inside, her sister was just coming down the stairs, dressed to go out.

'Hi, Sabrina,' she said briefly. 'Any luck on the job front?'

'Um, well, yes, actually,' Sabrina said guardedly. 'But it may only be temporary, for a few weeks. I'll see how my new boss and I get on. He's a writer,' she added, not bothering to mention his name. She went into the kitchen to put the kettle on. 'Are you just off to your aerobics class?'

'Yes—and I had a phone call this morning asking me to take over two dance classes later on—the usual girl has gone down with something—so I won't be home until about eight o'clock.'

The two girls were not very much alike to look at; Melinda was tall, dark-haired and brown-eyed with strong facial features, while Sabrina was only five-foot-three with a more delicate bone-structure and widely spaced eyes.

'I'm making something hot for our dinner,' Sabrina said, pouring boiling water into her mug. 'Will lasagne and salad do?'

'Brilliant,' Melinda said, going out and slamming the front door behind her.

Staring thoughtfully out of the window as she sipped her tea, Sabrina cast her mind back to the morning's interview, and to her new employer. To her, he seemed the typically self-assured alpha male, exuding British masculinity with just a hint of ruthlessness somewhere. There was also a brooding, slightly mysterious air about him, as if behind those black, magnetic eyes there was a tantalizing secret he'd never share with another human being.

She realized that she knew nothing at all of his past, whether he was, or had ever been married. In the press or society magazines, she'd never seen him pictured with a female in tow. His brother seemed to be the Lothario of the piece, frequently seen surrounded by pretty women.

Sabrina narrowed her eyes as her thoughts ran on, her analytical mind informing her that Alexander McDonald undoubtedly had a many-layered personality which wasn't necessarily going to be easy to cope with. She shrugged inwardly. The money he was offering would be a powerful incentive to keep her head down and do as he demanded.

Later, as Sabrina was frying the steak for their lasagne, her mobile rang and, frowning, she went across to answer it. She hoped it wasn't Melly in some sort of fix.

The dark tones which reached her ears made her senses rush. 'Miss Gold? Alexander McDonald here…' As if she needed telling! 'I was just thinking, there are still two working days left in the week—could you start earlier than we agreed? Like tomorrow?'

Without stopping to think, Sabrina said, 'Yes—I think so. Yes, all right, Mr McDonald.' He didn't need to know that she'd actually intended to go in to town to buy one or two things to add to her wardrobe. She hadn't been shopping for a while but, tough, he'd have to accept her as she was with not much of this year's fashion on show.

'Good—about nine, or earlier if you like,' he said. Then the phone went dead and Sabrina stared at the instrument for a second. Well, that was brief and to the point, she thought.

Back at number thirteen, Alexander leaned against his desk, a glass of whisky in his hands. He couldn't explain it, but he definitely had a good feeling about this new employee. There was something no-nonsense about her that appealed to him, besides a few other things, he acknowledged, remembering her candid green eyes, her neat hairstyle, her short, unpolished fingernails… And the soft, rather pleasing tone of her voice—a voice that wouldn't get on his nerves.

Still, all that mattered was whether her work proved to come up to his exacting standards, he thought, and that she'd be prepared to work a very long day when necessary.

Mulling over his interview with Sabrina Gold again, he realized that she was going to be very different from Janet. For one thing, Janet was a grandmother obsessed with her family and their new babies, while Sabrina was young and, from what he'd gathered from their conversation, lived with a sister, free of any emotional ties. That had to be a good thing, he thought—no commitments which might stand in the way of her work and their business association.

Feeling restless, as he often did when beginning to reach the end of a novel, he decided to go for a stroll before settling back down to do some more work later.

It was a delightfully soft, still, warm evening as he wandered along the pavement towards the local park at the end of the road, and he suddenly thought nostalgically of his wonderful home in France. With some luck he could arrange to be there by the end of October. He'd only managed two quick visits so far this year, he reminded himself ruefully, so he might even try and stay on over Christmas this time. That thought definitely appealed, because it would mean avoiding family and all the tedious *joie de vivre* that always took over the festive season. He could make the excuse that he was already committed to his next book and needed space and solitude.

His luxurious place abroad filled his mind. It was a large converted barn, standing almost alone amongst vines and olive groves, and in his absence safely watched over by his near-neighbours Marcel and Simone. Its large swimming pool, always warm and soothing, was surrounded by an expansive patio where on placid evenings he and some local friends would share freshly baked baguettes, sip wine from local vineyards, savour home-grown olives steeped in garlic-flavoured oil and just talk and let time slip by.

It was nearly dark as he wandered, lost in thought, through the almost-deserted park. He nearly fell over a courting couple lying on the grass. He stepped away quickly, muttering an awkward apology. But he needn't have bothered. They were oblivious to anything but themselves, their intertwined bodies and audible cries demonstrating the erotic pleasure of their coupling.

For some reason which he couldn't explain, a peculiar sadness came over Alexander for a few seconds. Those two were so young, so in love. He looked back to his own youth and the women he'd known. It seemed such a long time ago, another time, another country. Why had he indulged in no-strings-attached affairs for so long? Why had he never wanted true commitment? Was he that selfish? Had his disastrous relationship with Angelica put him off for ever? For heaven's sake, that was nearly ten years ago.

When he got back home he poured a fresh glass of whisky, then flung himself down on his bed. Ten minutes' sleep would do him good, he thought, before he returned to the study and perhaps the conclusion of that penultimate chapter which was worrying him.

Almost immediately, he fell into a deep sleep. A sleep filled with unbelievably colourful dreams which made his head move restlessly from side to side, his lips forming incomprehensible murmurings.

He was lying naked beside the beautiful, unclothed body of a woman. To his amazed delight, she was responding to his passionate advances with uninhibited ardour as she encouraged him to caress her body, her slender limbs, her cool, smooth breasts... When he knelt over her and possessed her completely, she parted her moist lips to receive the warmth of his mouth, the urgent thrust of his tongue…

Suddenly, he awoke and sprang up into a sitting position, his brow beaded with sweat. What the hell was that all about? What had set those particular bells ringing? This wasn't like him! He couldn't begin to remember the last time his emotions had been stirred with such an erotic, white-hot passion, either consciously or subconsciously.

Swinging his legs over the side of the bed, he stripped off his clothes and went into the bathroom. What he needed now was a long, very cold shower, he told himself.

Because in that so-immediate dream, the woman he had been making such intense love to had been unmistakable. She had been small with long, fair hair, unpolished fingernails and green, green eyes like those of an enchanting cat.

CHAPTER TWO

JUST after eight o'clock the following morning, wearing black trousers and a grey-and-white pin-striped shirt, Sabrina found herself standing once again outside number thirteen. Just as she was about to ring the bell, the door was thrust open and she came face to face with a short, grey-haired, middle-aged woman who was just coming out of the house, a couple of carrier bags in her hands.

'Oh, hi…' Sabrina began uncertainly, and the woman moved back for the girl to enter.

'Miss Gold? Ah. Mr McDonald left a note saying I might see you. I'm Maria, his daily—or his three-times-a-week, I should say.' She smiled. 'I haven't seen him this morning. He isn't up yet—probably getting over a heavy night!'

'Oh, I see,' Sabrina said, slightly taken aback. From yesterday's phone call, she'd imagined him to be an early riser. Shouldn't he already be hard at work and ready to spell out his instructions for the day?

'Anyway, go on up to the study—he said you knew where it was,' Maria said. 'I don't expect he'll be too long. By the way, the kitchen's just along there in the hall, first door on the right. Have some coffee, why don't you?' She paused, smiling again. 'Make yourself at home—and good luck!'

With that, Maria departed, leaving Sabrina feeling like some sort of intruder.

She decided against making herself acquainted with Alexander McDonald's kitchen just yet. Anyway, she'd had her usual light breakfast of cereal, yoghurt and honey and wouldn't need any coffee for a while. There was no sound at all in the house and for some reason Sabrina felt distinctly embarrassed to think of her employer tucked up in bed. As she trod lightly up the stairs, she wondered which room he was still sleeping in, whether it was one of those on the next floor. Trying to contain her thoughts, she reached his study and went inside.

The place was a total shambles. The rug on the floor had been pushed at a slightly drunken angle, and numerous books on the desk were scattered everywhere haphazardly, only just making room for three empty, stained coffee-mugs. Two baskets on the floor alongside were full of crumpled, screwed-up paper, and there seemed to be dust everywhere; Sabrina could see its lazy motes moving and shifting in the shafts of strong sunlight streaming in from the windows. She made a face to herself. This room was obviously out of bounds to Maria, she thought. It also felt over-warm and stuffy; impulsively she went over and unlatched one of the windows, throwing it wide open to let in some fresh air. She didn't know how long she would survive in this atmosphere.

Glancing down, she saw that the long, narrow garden was laid out in a strip of lawn, and here and there were clusters of stone pots filled with bright-red geraniums.

'Good morning.'

Alexander's voice made her turn quickly—she hadn't heard him come in—and immediately her pulse quickened as she looked up at him. He was wearing chinos and a black shirt, his hair roughly brushed and still damp from his shower. His face was unshaven, the line of dark stubble along his chin drawing Sabrina's helpless gaze to the seductive black hair just visible beneath his open-necked shirt. He came over to stand next to her and stared down, his dark, sensuous eyes trapping her enquiring green ones for a second.

'Sorry I wasn't here to greet you on your first morning,' he said, swallowing. The memory of last night's fantasy was still vivid, and uppermost in his mind. How was he going to rid himself of it and act normally? he thought briefly. He straightened his shoulders.

'I didn't get to bed until very late last night—well, it was early this morning, actually,' he added. 'But I have to keep going until I'm satisfied that I've got things right, whatever the hour. Not that it worked this time, I'm afraid,' he added.

Sabrina frowned briefly, not knowing how to respond to that remark. She moved away from him and went towards her own desk.

'Well, sometimes a new day can bring fresh ideas?' she suggested, cross at the way her cheeks had flushed at being alone with Alexander McDonald. She hadn't felt this way yesterday at the interview. But that was different. Then she had employed all her clinical instincts to get what she wanted—this job. It had kept her cool, calm and rational, deflecting her thoughts from any other feelings she might experience at being in close proximity to one of the most lusted-after—and apparently elusive—men on the London scene.

But this morning realization set in. She was going

to be closeted in this room with him for many hours for the foreseeable future, and once again Sabrina felt threatened and in danger of becoming emotionally affected by a member of the opposite sex. She didn't need her professional qualifications to work that one out, yet she was quietly horrified. Hadn't fate's cruel hand made her decide to stick to work and to the needs of her sister from now on, for all time? She was not going to allow life ever again to bring her to the dizzy heights of supreme happiness, only to dash her to the ground and break her heart into pieces.

She should have been married to Stephen by now, but in a tragic, mad moment destiny had taken over. Stephen had lost his life in a friendly rugby-game, never regaining consciousness from a one-in-a-million chance accident on the pitch.

Sabrina had considered herself the luckiest woman in the world when he'd asked her to marry him. Not just because he was so good-looking, with the most amazing deep-gold hair with eyes to match, but because he was funny, loyal and kind. He had promised Sabrina that Melly would always have a home with them, for as long as she needed it. Life had been so good—too good to be true. How many other men would have understood the sense of responsibility towards her sister made so acute by the family background? Their father had walked out a long time ago, and their mother, Philippa, had remarried when the girls were in their teens and at their most vulnerable. She was now living in Sydney with her husband, and rarely came back to the UK, confining her interest in her daughters to somewhat irregular phone-calls. So everything that had happened had made Sabrina feel as if she really was left holding the baby—and knowing with absolute certainty that now she'd never hold one of her own. Because she'd never trust love again, never risk losing again, and she'd managed to convince herself that her need for a man, any man to share her existence, had died for ever.

Yet the burgeoning rush to her senses now told its own story. It was undeniable that Alexander McDonald was seducing her—in thought, if not in deed! It was hardly his fault, but it was the worst possible scenario for a successful business-arrangement, so she'd better get a grip and keep any wayward thoughts well under wraps, she told herself.

Alexander pushed back the chair by his desk and sat down heavily, glancing down with some distaste at the disorderly mess in front of him.

'I should at least have washed up these mugs before I eventually went to bed,' he said. He glanced across at Sabrina. 'Do sit, Miss Gold.'

Sabrina didn't sit down, returning his glance squarely. 'I hope you'll call me Sabrina,' she said, thinking almost immediately that maybe Alexander McDonald preferred to be more formal with his staff.

But straight away he said, 'Good. And I'm usually known as Alex. So at least we've cleared something up this morning.'

He smiled across at her briefly, his full lips parting to expose white, immaculate teeth. Desperately trying to rein in her imagination—and failing once again— Sabrina fleetingly wondered what it would feel like to have that sensuous mouth close in on hers. He was impossibly handsome, she thought, as his blue-black eyes searched her face. Yet Sabrina was aware that there was a hint of something more behind Alexander's overtly masculine features, his obviously desirable appearance. There was something about him that both excited and intrigued her. She tried to stem the annoying tingling at the back of her neck, and as he continued scrutinizing her Sabrina had the uncomfortable feeling that he was reading her mind. She certainly hoped not. She tore her eyes from his penetrating gaze, clearing her throat.

'Do you have any sort of set plan for me…to make a beginning?' she said tentatively, glancing around and wondering where on earth they were going to start. She hoped she wasn't expected to come up with any brilliant ideas for the current project he seemed to be having difficulty with. She'd never tried her hand at creative writing, though she'd always been an avid reader from as far back as she could remember. Alexander McDonald's books were known to be serious and highly literary tomes, and from what she'd read in the book reviews his plots were strong, often dark and with no happy endings guaranteed. They were not really her own choice of reading matter at the end of a working day spent trying to unravel troubled lives and situations for her patients. She wondered briefly when she'd be able to return to her own profession.

'Have you ever read any of my books?' Alexander asked bluntly, desperately trying not to keep looking at her. Sabrina coloured up again; he *was* reading her mind! She paused for only a fraction of a second.

'No—I haven't,' she said simply. 'I have read *about* your books in all the reviews, and they seem…somewhat heavier material than I can cope with.' She hesitated. 'My normal reading time is an hour or so before I go to sleep,' she explained. 'And what I need then is total relaxation, a distraction. I mean, I wouldn't want to be thinking, dreaming, worrying about all your characters, to have them on my mind all night.'

There was a moment's silence after that and Sabrina

hoped she hadn't put a nail in her own coffin. If she wasn't careful this could turn out to be a very short-term employment. She didn't think Alexander McDonald appreciated criticism—or, worse, a lack of interest—especially from someone like her.

But she couldn't have been more wrong, because she was treated once more to a brief, heart-wrenching smile as he looked at her, his eyes narrowing. The woman might have said she'd read everything he'd ever written and that she considered it all wonderful, he thought. But she'd been honest enough to say she'd never even read the first page of any of his books.

He got up and came around to stand in front of his desk, leaning casually against it and staring down at her.

'Good. That means you've got no preconceived ideas. Your opinion on something that may be a sticking point for me is going to be invaluable.' He paused. 'Janet—my faithful secretary for the last fifteen years—was a useful contributor in this way now and again, but lately it had become a matter of her trying to please me, to tell me what she thought I wanted to hear. That's no good.' He thrust his hands into his pockets. 'It was something of a relief when she decided to retire.'

Sabrina swallowed, biting her lip. By the sound of it, this job was certainly not going to be stereotypical, as he'd made clear from the start. But she'd not envisaged it including her having to offer her opinion on the esteemed writing of one of the most successful authors in the world. But then, she thought, she'd read most of the classics—read and re-read them—and was a regular visitor to the library and bookshops, keeping up with all the modern output. Maybe she'd be some use after all, in a small way. She wanted to be useful to Alexander

McDonald. And it might prove to be an interesting diversion for her.

He turned around now, picking up a large diary and handing it over to Sabrina

'This is an essential part of my life,' he said. 'And from now on, you're in charge of it, Sabrina. I need you to remind me at frequent intervals what's coming up and where I'm meant to be, and who with. I tend to be forgetful most of the time.' He moved beside her, flicking the pages over. 'Oh, and I would rather you always answer the telephone—just tell the caller to hold while I decide whether I want to talk or not. If I do, I'll pick up my extension; if not, I'll give you the thumbs down and you can think up some excuse.'

For the next hour, Sabrina listened as he explained how he liked everything done, and learned that he didn't like things moved about unnecessarily. 'If you tidy up too much, we'll never remember where anything is,' he said flatly, and Sabrina smiled inwardly. She'd been right in thinking that Maria wasn't welcome here. She threw discretion to the winds; she did have some requests of her own.

'Am I at least allowed to clean some dust from my desk—and from yours?' she said. She feigned a dainty sneeze. 'It would be advantageous for both of us,' she added.

He shrugged, as if the matter of dust had never entered his head. 'Feel free,' he said casually.

Finally, she was handed an A4 note pad with pages full of scribbled writing.

'Type this up and print it out, will you? See if you can make sense of my scrawl.'

Sabrina took a long, deep breath, feeling upbeat for a moment. She knew she could handle this job, because she wanted to, desperately. Twenty-four hours ago she hadn't even met Alexander McDonald, but she owned up again to a feeling of warmth towards him. He seemed quite nice, as new bosses went, though it was obvious to her that he might be touchy at times. Well, she could handle touchy, she thought.

They were standing close together now, their heads bent over the script they were looking at. His tall frame made Sabrina feel tiny, insignificant and distinctly shivery as he towered above her, the titillating musk of his bronzed skin reaching her nostrils. As he turned another page, their hands touched briefly and Sabrina was painfully aware of his long, sensitive fingers.

She moved away from him slightly, trying to keep her mind from intrusive thoughts, and went across to boot up her computer, thinking that all that writing didn't look too impossible to interpret, but it was full of alterations and crossings-out which would take time to sort. She bit her lip, feeling that the worst part of the job was the fact that she and her employer were going to be here in this room together all the time. She'd much rather have an office of her own—a decent cupboard would do—where she wouldn't feel those eyes judging her, assessing her every move. Surely he'd go out sometimes and leave her in peace?

Reading her thoughts, as usual, he said, 'I'm due at the gym for a couple of hours this morning. But first I'm going to make us some coffee.'

Sabrina stood up. Surely making the coffee was one of the duties of his personal assistant? 'I'll do it,' she said quickly. 'Maria showed me where the kitchen is.'

He nodded, walking towards the door and glancing back at her. 'OK,' he said, relieved that he was feeling more in charge of himself by this time. 'And I might as well show you the domestic side of things straight away. We may need to make ourselves something to eat at the end of a long day.'

He led the way down the stairs and along the hall to the kitchen, Sabrina following in his wake. She remembered him saying yesterday that he would expect her to stay on after normal working hours when necessary, and she shrugged inwardly. She'd do whatever it took to keep this highly lucrative position. Her expression clouded briefly as she remembered how low Melly had been this morning when she'd looked in on her in her bedroom.

The kitchen was large, immaculate and welcoming. There was a spotless Aga, a large refectory table and chairs. Holding prime position in the centre of the room was a double oven with overhead lighting and shining granite surfaces. *Goodness me*, Sabrina thought, *what does he need all these facilities for when he is the only occupant of the house?* Perhaps he was always entertaining, she thought, though somehow that didn't seem likely. She sighed inwardly, thinking of her own small kitchen that was badly in need of a refit.

Alexander threw open the door of one of the cupboards. 'Everything you may need is here, or in the fridge,' he said, looking back at her. 'Maria does all my shopping, makes sure I don't run out of essentials—though I do eat out rather a lot.' He paused. 'I've become adept at scrambling eggs, and that's just about it.'

Sabrina smiled up at him briefly and went over to the sink to fill the kettle.

'I'll go and get changed and come back in a minute for my coffee—which I like black,' Alexander said. 'And feel free to help yourself to anything you want, whether I'm here or not,' he added.

Sabrina set out the things she needed, putting coffee granules into the cafetière, and was just reaching for two mugs when the telephone rang. She frowned. It wasn't the land line, it was a mobile, and it certainly wasn't hers. Then she saw that Alexander had left his on one of the surfaces, and she went over to answer it. Before she could open her mouth, a woman's rather strident tones filled her ears.

'Alexander? You have not been returning my calls. That is extremely naughty of you!'

'Excuse me,' Sabrina said hastily. 'Um, I'll see if Mr McDonald is in.'

There was a second's pause. 'Is that Janet?' the voice demanded.

'No, I'm Mr McDonald's new secretary,' Sabrina said. 'Janet does not work for him now.'

'*Really?* He didn't tell me anything about getting a new secretary,' the voice said in a rather complaining tone. 'Oh, well. I want to speak to him, please.'

'I'll see if he's in,' Sabrina repeated. 'May I ask who's calling?'

'This is *Lydia*,' the voice said, as if that should have been obvious to anyone with half a brain cell.

'One moment,' Sabrina said, putting the phone down carefully and leaving the room, running up the stairs two at a time. Alexander was just coming out of one of the rooms dressed in a white T-shirt and shorts, his brown, muscular thighs and calves shadowed with dark hair. He was looking so unutterably seductive that Sabrina almost forgot what she was supposed to be doing.

'There's a call on your mobile—which you left in the kitchen,' she faltered.

'Oh, I'm always mislaying the wretched thing,' he said. 'Who wants to speak to me?'

'Someone called Lydia,' Sabrina replied, turning to go back down the stairs.

He didn't reply to that, but followed Sabrina into the kitchen and picked up the phone.

'Good morning, Lydia,' he said casually. Before he could utter another word, Sabrina could hear those distinctive tones sailing on uninterrupted.

'Why haven't you been returning my calls?' the woman said petulantly. 'It really is most annoying, Alexander.'

'Yes, I know. Sorry, Lydia.' He paused. 'It's just that I've been extremely busy, and rather distracted, because Janet has left and I've had to find someone else suitable.'

'Yes, I've just been told about Janet,' the woman went on. 'Your problem is you work too hard, Alexander. Anyway, enough about all that. I hope you're still free for Sunday week?'

As Sabrina poured the boiling water onto the coffee, she couldn't help being riveted to the conversation going on beside her. Alexander made no effort to exclude her from listening in. Who was Lydia? Clearly an over-familiar lady friend who didn't seem very important to Alexander, if the expression on his face was anything to go by.

'Sunday week?' he repeated, frowning.

'Yes, Sunday week,' the woman said. 'Look, I'm not taking no for an answer this time, Alexander.' She paused. 'There are going to be lots of party people there you'll know.'

'I don't do parties. You know that, Lydia,' he said.

'You always used to! Your...social reputation was very well-known at one time.'

'That was a *very* long while ago, Lydia,' Alexander

replied. 'I have, shall we say, outgrown parties.'
Especially your parties, he thought. 'I really do not find
them entertaining any more.'

'Well, I can promise you that you'll find this one
entertaining,' Lydia persisted. 'Do say you'll come?'

Alexander glanced at Sabrina, raising his eyebrows
in mild exasperation.

'Oh, well, OK. If you insist, Lydia,' he said at last.
'I'll do my best.'

'Wonderful! And, by the way, Lucinda is back in
England and she'll be at the party.' There was a long
pause. 'She particularly asked whether you were going
to be there when we spoke on the phone. Mentioned
something about an old score to settle.'

Alexander's mouth turned down at the corners. 'I
wonder whether Lucinda and I will recognize each
other,' he said. 'After all this time.'

There was a girlish giggle at the other end. 'I doubt
that there will be *any* difficulty with that. You were *very
close* once, weren't you?'

'That also was a very long time ago, Lydia,' Alexander
said, clearly irritated by now. 'Um, look, I have to go.
But thanks for the call.'

'Don't forget—Sunday the sixteenth. And don't be
late!' was the parting shot.

He ended the call and Alexander turned to pick up
his coffee, glancing down at Sabrina, his eyes narrowing
slightly.

After a moment he said thoughtfully, 'Could you
possibly arrange to be available on the evening of the
sixteenth to come to this function it seems I can't get out
of?' He paused. 'It might be useful to have you there.'
He cleared his throat. 'I'm sorry it's a Sunday, when

I wouldn't normally ask you to work, but it would be helpful if you could.'

Sabrina frowned thoughtfully. She hadn't realized how demanding this job was going to be, but if needs must she'd better do as her employer wanted. She made a mental note to bring a note pad and pen with her.

'When I get home I'll double check I'm free,' she said. 'But I think I can do as you ask.'

'Great. Thanks.' He finished his coffee and turned to go. 'I very rarely see my mother these days, and sometimes I just have to fall in with her wishes.'

'Your mother?'

'Yes—Lydia. My mother,' Alexander said as he left the room.

CHAPTER THREE

By THE middle of the following week, Sabrina felt she was beginning to get to grips with her secretarial duties, starting with the countless pieces of mail which arrived in the post each morning, and fielding all the telephone calls—most of which Alexander refused to follow up.

'They're always about being asked to go places, attend functions,' he grumbled once, as she showed him the list. 'Can't be bothered.'

After Alexander had left to go to the gym the previous Thursday, Sabrina had concentrated on trying to decipher his terrible handwriting. Bit by bit she had managed to unravel the meaning of the subtle and sophisticated prose, all of it, naturally, in perfect English—even if his spelling didn't quite match up. She even felt privileged to have sight of it, to be the first to read this particular new piece, to share the inner workings of his illustrious mind.

But more of those warning bells began to ring for her when, after a particularly poignant page or two, Sabrina had found herself stopping to trace the script gently with her forefinger, as if by touching the words he'd written she was touching him. Getting close. How dreadful was that? Alexander McDonald was arousing dangerous feelings in her which she thought she'd ruled out for ever.

By Friday afternoon she was able to hand him the countless pages, everything he'd asked her to type up, and he seemed genuinely pleased with the result.

'Thanks very much,' he said later, after scrutinizing each page carefully. 'That even makes some sense to me now.' He shot Sabrina a quick glance, thinking his new secretary had cottoned on to his requirements quicker than he'd dared to hope.

One thing which Sabrina was grateful for was that Alexander went to the gym on Tuesday and Thursday mornings, so she did have some time when he wasn't sitting a few feet away from her. He'd also been away on two occasions for meetings with his agent. It was so much easier to concentrate when she was by herself— especially as several times when they'd been together she'd looked across briefly to see him watching her, one finely arched eyebrow raised thoughtfully, his perfect, sensuous lips parted slightly. Sabrina had coloured immediately, a surging tide of feeling seeping down to her groin.

Sensing her discomfiture, Alexander had said hurriedly, 'I was admiring the speed at which you type, Sabrina. I can never manage more than one finger at a time.'

'Well, what I do is the easy bit. I mean, where does all this come from, or start from, Alexander? I mean, *Alex*?' she'd asked, feeling uncomfortable at using his Christian name. 'How on earth do you compose such intricate and beautiful work?'

'With the utmost difficulty, most of the time,' he'd replied. 'Someone once said that writing was the same as hacking lumps out of granite—and it often feels like that.'

'Well, you'd never know it from this,' Sabrina had said, meaning it. 'All these words which I've typed seem to just spill off the paper, like oil running from a spoon.'

He had seemed pleasantly surprised at that. 'Does that mean you might even read one of my books one day?' he'd said, only half-teasing. She'd looked up at him, hoping she hadn't said the wrong thing or been over-familiar with her boss.

But Sabrina readily admitted that in the short time she'd known him he'd appeared far less demanding than she might have expected. There'd certainly been no evidence of the moodiness he'd hinted at during the interview. But it was early days. Perhaps this was the calm before the storm.

The thing which she was dreading was Sunday evening being spent with Lydia, and it seemed a host of other people as well, none of whom Sabrina would know. To hang around for hours with a load of complete strangers, not to mention her very new boss, wasn't exactly an enticing thought. Why had Alexander asked her to go with him, anyway? Surely he'd find her a hindrance? What would be expected of her? Thinking about it again, she shrugged inwardly. However boring she found it, it could only last a few hours, and the almost outrageous rate which Alexander was paying her to do his every bidding should be compensation enough.

Now, with the end of her first full week in sight, Sabrina looked across at Alexander as he sat bent over the desk with his head in one hand and scribbling furiously with the other. Her heart missed a beat or two as she watched him silently, unable to resist her body's reaction to the powerful sexuality he exuded. It wasn't just his achingly seductive appearance, it was something far deeper and totally indefinable.

Alexander McDonald should wear a warning notice around his neck, Sabrina thought: *to all females everywhere: danger. Keep away.* Clearly, he had no wish to be tied down to any female, otherwise he should surely be committed to someone by now. But his single status was a well-known phenomenon, and was an occasional topic in the gossip magazines. As she continued studying him thoughtfully, Sabrina felt she was beginning to understand him a bit. He was obviously married to his work, she thought, and living his life through his characters. That was what steered him through. And it was enough.

'Are you going to make some tea?' he asked suddenly without looking up. With a rush of self-consciousness, Sabrina wondered if he'd known she'd been gazing across at him.

'Yes. I was just going to do that,' she said, getting up and leaving the room.

In the kitchen, she was just filling the kettle when her mobile rang and she took it from her jeans pocket, frowning briefly. It could only be Melly.

It was, and the girl's excitable voice almost deafened Sabrina as she listened.

'Sabrina? You'll never guess! You know those dancing classes I took over at short notice because the girl was ill? Well, they've asked me to step in again, only this time it's something much more exciting!'

'Go on, tell me,' Sabrina said patiently.

'I've been asked to go to Spain! To teach at a summer school—well, an autumn school, really. And it's a two-week contract to include musical theatre, aerobics and dance, and I think some singing as well. People have enrolled from all over the place to take part, and participants, as well as those of us who'll be running the classes, will all be put up at various houses. Everything's taken care of, Sabrina. All I need is to take my clothes and passport—oh, and some money, of course—and turn up on Sunday morning when the minibus will be taking us to Heathrow!'

Melly hardly paused for breath, not giving Sabrina a chance to interrupt. 'It's a wonderful opportunity, Sabrina—and I know two of the teachers who are going. They've done this sort of thing before and they say it's fantastic fun, and a holiday as well—all expenses paid—and we get a respectable cheque for our services at the end! What do you think?'

Well, what *could* Sabrina think or say other than to join in her sister's enthusiasm? 'Bring home all the necessary literature for us to check out, Melly,' she said reasonably. 'But I should think it will be perfectly OK. Though I'm sure you'll have to work pretty hard for your holiday!' She bit her lip, hoping that Melly wouldn't suffer from any depression during the proposed assignment. Her attacks were so unpredictable, and she'd be too far away for Sabrina to help her.

'Oh, I know that. There will be several sessions each day, but time for breaks as well.' There was a pause at the other end. 'The only thing is, I don't have much money at the moment—as you know, Sabrina—so could you lend me a bit? I'll be able to repay you when I get home.'

'Oh, don't worry about the money, I'll sort that out,' Sabrina said, suddenly elated at her sister's news. This could be stimulating for Melly, she thought, a complete change—and a much-needed boost to her confidence.

* * *

Early on Sunday morning, Sabrina waved the minibus out of sight. She was thinking that, if nothing else came from this experience for her sister, it was going to be the first break away from her, Sabrina, and from home, for a very long time.

She sighed briefly, biting her lip as she watched the bus disappear around the corner, before walking back the short distance to where she'd parked the car. Melly was twenty-six years old, after all. Yet she was the kid sister, vulnerable and easily hurt, her fragile emotional state often rocked by outside influences. Sabrina fervently hoped that this trip would turn out to be everything Melly thought it would be, with no complications.

Sabrina did feel relieved to have met the leader of the excursion this morning—a youngish man called Sam—who'd reassured her that everyone would be in safe hands and that these events were always well organized.

Driving slowly back home, Sabrina tried to think about this evening and how she was going to get through it. She had not liked the sound of Lydia one little bit. And how strange that Alexander called his mother by her Christian name—what was that all about? Perhaps that was what elevated people did, she thought idly. Then something else struck her: what should she wear to this do? Alexander hadn't given her a clue about any of it; his only directive as they'd parted company on Friday was that she must be ready when he arrived to pick her up at seven o'clock.

Still, she thought now as she parked outside their modest front gate, her black dress would have to be her salvation again, her suitable-for-anywhere item. It was well-cut, of good-quality material and wearing it always made her feel sure of herself, confident. If she kept it plain and didn't deck it out with any jewellery, it could be classed as a perfect number for her role as secretary to Alexander McDonald. Not that he would bother about what she was wearing, or even notice what she had on, Sabrina thought.

The traffic that evening was abnormally heavy, and it had gone eight by the time Alexander drove his sleek, bronze Aston Martin slowly up the wide approach to his parents' mansion, set in the Surrey countryside.

As Sabrina peered ahead at the imposing building, she saw lights from every open window shining out like beacons. As reverberating waves of high-pitched chatting and loud laughter could easily be heard, she felt like jumping out of the car and running away. But that thought lasted for less than a second as she remembered who she was with, who her employer was, and she hardened her resolve to be the perfect personal assistant to Alexander McDonald. To be ready for anything he might need her for, and to remain professional and businesslike.

The huge oak door was thrown open by a uniformed maid, who ushered them straight away into a brightly lit room, which to Sabrina seemed to stretch almost out of sight. There must be more than a hundred people present, she thought, realizing in those first few seconds that everyone seemed extravagantly dressed.

Alexander, his dark eyes sweeping the scene at a glance, knew he'd been right in not wanting to be here. It was one of his mother's usual parties, he thought with distaste, where she invited just about everyone she knew—many of them young women, some not so young, who laughed too loudly and drank too much. His perceptive gaze had already spotted two whom he knew to be immensely rich, thanks to the well-known escort agencies they owned and ran in town.

Putting his hand lightly on Sabrina's arm, he guided her across the room towards the long, white-clothed table laden with alcohol of every description. Before he could pour either of them a drink, the easily recognizable voice of Lydia reached Sabrina's ears as the woman bore down on them.

She was wearing a three-quarter-length sheath dress in a brilliant purple colour, and its smooth, satiny material perfectly accentuated her hour-glass figure. Her silver hair was an elegant, shining knot on her head, her sculpted lips painted a bright glossy red. Alexander's mother was certainly a very handsome woman who had clearly passed on her looks to her son. Her arms outstretched in welcome, she embraced Alexander carefully, offering him her cheek and making sure her make-up was not disturbed.

'Alexander! Darling! I was afraid you weren't going to turn up!'

Yes, mother dearest, I know exactly how that feels, he thought cynically, remembering the countless times his mother had not bothered to turn up at the regular boarding-school events to which parents were always invited. Remembering how he'd kept on hoping, until the very last minute, that she'd arrive. But she'd clearly felt that her maternal obligations ended the moment her sons left home at the tender age of seven; she had never left them in any doubt about that.

Alexander could recall her exact words as she'd waved him off on that first day.

'Remember, Alexander,' she'd said, 'that you are no longer a child—and you must accept responsibility for yourself.' She'd paused only briefly. 'And from now on

I want to be known as Lydia, not Mummy—do you understand? Mummy is a silly, childish word.'

'But when I write to you can't I put "dear Mummy"?' Alexander had asked earnestly.

'Certainly not,' his mother had replied. 'Someone might see it. Just put "dear Lydia". That is my name, after all.'

Staring down at his mother now, Alexander realized that he and Bruno, who was two years his senior, had never discussed the matter but had accepted their mother's directive without question. At least their father, Angus, had made no such demands and was always affectionately known as Dad. The older man didn't seem to be here tonight, Alexander noticed, but that was nothing new. Their parents had lived separate lives for years.

'Yes—a lot of traffic, I'm afraid,' Alexander said, in answer to his mother's remark.

'Never mind, you're here now. Though, of course, Bruno is otherwise engaged this evening—what's new?' Lydia sighed with a little pout. 'A heavy meeting with some influential new backers, apparently. Still, there are *masses* of your friends here tonight, all desperate to see you again. It's been too long since you've been circulating; someone said it's as if you've disappeared off the face of the planet!'

'Well, I hope this evening will lay that supposition to rest,' Alexander said flatly. He paused, flickering a glance at Sabrina. 'As I'm aware that your guest list is always flexible, Lydia,' he went on, 'I've brought someone along with me tonight—my personal assistant, Sabrina. Janet's replacement,' he added.

Sabrina was only too aware that Alexander's mother had barely noticed she was there at all—or, if she had, she'd chosen to ignore it.

The woman turned now to look briefly at Sabrina. 'Oh yes, I remember speaking to you on the telephone,' she said dismissively. 'How do you do?' she added as an afterthought. Then she took hold of Alexander's arm firmly. 'Now, come along,' she said. 'Dinner is going to be served in half an hour, so you've a little time to catch up with everyone first.'

Alexander's lips set in a hard line as he deliberately prised his mother's hand away from him. 'All in good time,' he said. 'Sabrina and I would like a drink first.'

'Well, don't be long,' Lydia said, waving to someone at the other end of the room. 'Look, there's Danielle, I must go and talk to her…' she said, moving away.

Waving briefly to several people who were calling out and wanting to gain his attention, Alexander poured out two glasses of white wine, handing one to Sabrina, and their eyes met for a second. He looked down at her thoughtfully, noticing for the first time that evening what she was wearing. The black dress she had on suited her dainty, curvaceous figure perfectly, he thought, and he liked her hair coiled up like that. It gave her a cool, elfin, distinctive look, and tonight those eyes which he found so fascinating seemed brighter and greener than ever. She wasn't wearing a scrap of jewellery or make-up, as far as he could tell, but why should she bother? She didn't need anything, her natural attributes were entirely sufficient.

Irritated at his own thoughts, and still looking at her, he took a drink from his glass. He didn't look at women any more, he reminded himself. Not in the way he always had. The youthful, carefree days of enjoying the pleasures of the opposite sex had long gone and the experience had taught him many things—uppermost of which was in future to steer clear of the sort of women he'd so often come in contact with. Vain and self-seeking, many of them were overtly promiscuous, leading little, brittle lives.

It had all made him realize, believe, that he didn't actually *like* women very much at all. He admired them, some of them; well, that was the male instinct and not his fault, he thought. But there had not been one in his past, apart from Angelica, whom he could imagine might have been prepared to settle down and be a faithful wife to someone like him, forced to spend so many hours in isolation as he worked. Nor to understand his moods when he became quiet and withdrawn sometimes, or that he didn't particularly like the heady London life and all that went with it.

He took another swig from his glass. One thing he was damned sure about—he would never find himself in the same wretched position as his father, providing untold wealth to a fickle and demanding partner who lived solely for her own gratification. His brow knitted briefly. His solitary state—though not always entirely fulfilling, he admitted—was at least comfortable. Sorting out the lives of the characters in his books was difficult enough, heaven only knew. To have a real life woman to deal with and to try to satisfy was never going to be one of his problems. He'd come to that decision a long time ago, and it was final.

Sabrina, realizing that he had been scrutinizing her for several moments, felt her cheeks begin to burn and she glanced up quickly. 'Are you expecting your agent to be here tonight?' she asked innocently. 'Or someone from your publisher's?' she added, wondering why she was there at all, what her role was to be.

'Good grief, no, I hope not!' Alexander said at once.

'No, this is just one of my mother's pointless parties, and I didn't particularly want to come to it alone, that's all.'

And that was the truth, he thought. It had been a somewhat impetuous act on his part to ask Sabrina to accompany him, but for some strange reason the thought that she would be there had made the prospect of the event slightly more acceptable. He shrugged inwardly. She was his personal assistant, after all, ready to do as he asked when the need arose, and she hadn't seemed to mind coming along. His brow furrowed again as he remembered Lydia's reaction when he'd introduced Sabrina just now. His mother had been totally uninterested to meet his new secretary—and was that such a surprise? Sabrina did not fit the mould of the women his mother had always liked being with.

Suddenly, like a minor earthquake approaching, three women rushed up and gathered around Alexander, all talking at once, and each embracing him effusively, almost making him spill his drink.

'Alex!' they chorused together. 'Long time, no see. Where have you been hiding?'

Alexander put his drink down on the table and looked at the women. 'Not hiding, just working,' he said blandly. 'How's everyone doing? I must say, you're all looking as lovely as ever.'

They all gushed their pleasure at that remark, and as they all began to babble on, each vying to make herself heard above the others, Sabrina stood back, fascinated to witness their over-exuberant behaviour— and to see Alexander's casually charming manner as he responded to everything they were saying. It was clear that they were absolutely besotted by the famous, handsome, reputedly unavailable Alexander McDonald. She looked away for a moment, feeling as if she was a voyeur witnessing a mating game. But what was also clear was that she herself hadn't even been noticed, nor the fact that Alexander had someone with him. Well, secretaries were supposed to make themselves invisible when the occasion demanded, she thought. It was as if she wasn't there at all as she was faced with the backs of the three extravagantly dressed women clustered around Alexander, still chattering non-stop.

After a few moments of this, he eased himself away and reached over to take Sabrina's arm.

'Sally, Debbie, Samantha—let me introduce you to my secretary, Sabrina,' he began, and for the first time the women turned, deigning to look at Sabrina, their faces blank.

Just as they were murmuring their polite greeting, another woman arrived and draped her arms around Alexander's neck. 'Alex,' she breathed. 'At last...'

'Hello, Lucinda,' he said, disentangling himself gently. 'You're looking wonderful, as usual.' He drew Sabrina into the gathering. 'Meet my new assistant, Sabrina.'

Lucinda was tall, raven-haired and swathed in a tight-fitting, low-cut red dress which left nothing to the imagination. She stared at Sabrina, a curious expression on her hard features.

'Oh. So what happened to funny, little, old dowdy Janet?' she said, turning to Alexander again. 'Did she die quietly at her desk?'

'Funny, little, old dowdy Janet, as you put it, decided that she'd had enough and is now spending much-deserved time with her family,' Alexander said, and Sabrina could see that the woman's remarks had angered him.

'Oh, so you're the new typist, then, are you?' Lucinda

said, looking down at Sabrina, her eyes taking in her appearance at a glance. 'I wonder how you'll put up with Alexander the Great?'

'I've had no difficulty so far,' Sabrina said neatly, suddenly rattled at the company she was in, and realizing that she herself had hardly uttered a word to anyone yet.

Lucinda shrugged. 'Efficient typists are difficult to find; I know *that* to my cost,' she said. 'Though I'm afraid secretarial work would drive me absolutely bonkers, *whoever* I was working for,' she added. 'I mean, any office work is deadly boring—surely only a stop-gap before finding other more intellectually fulfilling occupations for the more intelligent among us?' She blinked, her false eyelashes sweeping her cheek. 'I run my own marketing company,' she drawled importantly. 'Which regularly keeps me out of the country. But I'm afraid my secretary in the London office comes under the heading of "brain dead". Lazy and utterly useless!'

The others all tittered at that, and Alexander cut in calmly, 'You've obviously lost your powers of discernment, Lucinda,' he said. 'I have no such problems. Janet was a loyal, hard-working, good-natured professional and was seldom away. She was with me for fifteen years.' He paused, glancing at Sabrina. 'And I very much hope that Sabrina will beat that,' he added, though thinking that that wasn't likely. Sabrina would want to return to her own line when the time was right.

Lucinda slipped her arm through Alexander's and held him to her. 'Oh, we don't want to waste time talking about boring work. Now, Alex, you do remember our little arrangement…?' she said eagerly.

The expression on Alexander's face told its own story

as he stared at the woman. He answered coolly, 'What arrangement was that?'

'Oh, you *must* remember, surely?' Lucinda cried.

'Bad luck, Lucinda,' the others laughed. 'We told you he wouldn't have given it another thought!'

'Then I'll remind you, Alex,' Lucinda persisted. 'We agreed that when I came back to the UK, if neither of us had, shall we say, settled down, we'd see what fate had in store for us. Remember now?'

'It was all a very long time ago, Lucinda,' Alexander said calmly, thinking, *and I only said that to keep you out of my face.*

'Well, *Lydia* has certainly not forgotten,' Lucinda said. She paused. 'Your mother has prepared the west wing for anyone who might need it tonight, Alex—who may prefer not to go home until tomorrow, I mean.' She looked up into Alexander's eyes. 'We'll be able to discuss things, Alex, be alone. It'll be like getting to know each other all over again.'

Sabrina felt herself go hot and cold with embarrassment at the unbridled talk going on over her head. Not embarrassed on her own behalf, but on Alexander's. But he merely shrugged his shoulders as if Lucinda had just given out the weather forecast.

'No can do, I'm afraid.' he said casually. 'It's always an early start on Mondays, and deadlines are deadlines.'

At that moment, Lydia came up to them, her face wreathed in smiles as she saw her son surrounded by adoring females. Totally ignoring Sabrina, she said, 'There, isn't this wonderful? There's nothing like a get-together with old friends!' She glanced at the expensive gold watch on her wrist. 'Dinner's being served, so come along, everyone—the night is young!'

Sabrina suddenly felt angry at the situation she was in, because it was being made absolutely clear that she was not really a guest. After all, Alexander hadn't even told his mother he was bringing her. Nothing so far had managed to put Sabrina at her ease. She was like a fish out of water. How *could* he have put her in this position, and not give a thought to her sensitivities?

By now the noise and forced gaiety in the over-crowded room was deafening, making Sabrina's head thump uncomfortably. Then she was aware that Lydia had moved next to her son, not bothering to keep her voice down.

'What on earth made you decide to bring some-one—that woman—with you tonight, Alexander?' she complained.

'Why—is there a problem?' he asked mildly.

'Yes, there is. I've naturally seated you at dinner with everyone you know,' she said firmly. 'I mean, I had no idea you were bringing anyone with you tonight, so your secretary Sabrina will have to take her place at the other end of the table. Will that do?'

Alexander waited a moment before replying, then said, 'No, I'm afraid it will not do, Lydia. For all sorts of reasons,' he added.

'Oh, *please* don't be difficult, Alexander,' Lydia said crossly. She didn't bother to lower her voice. 'The wom-an's your secretary—or your personal whatever-she-is; describe it as you will. She's not…she's not one of our crowd, is she? Surely she won't expect to be included among our inner circle?'

Not if she's got any sense, Alexander thought. He moved closer to Sabrina who, amongst this highly coloured crowd, looked to him like a desirable goddess.

Suddenly, energized into action, Sabrina spoke up, her voice clear and authoritative. She looked at Lydia squarely.

'There is no need for you to concern yourself about me,' she said. 'In fact, I don't feel like anything to eat.' She paused. 'But allow me to apologize—on Alexander's behalf—that I'm here at all, and that you were not informed that I was coming to your home to-night. Uninvited guests are seldom welcome.'

She chose not to look at Alexander, but if she had he'd have been in no doubt what her feelings were. He'd had no right to bring her with him; she hadn't wanted to come, and she wasn't wanted. He'd have the benefit of her opinion later, she thought grimly, angry colour flooding her cheeks once more.

Despite Lydia's earlier protestations, a seat next to Alexander was found for Sabrina, and in a few minutes everyone was seated at the impressive table waiting to be served. Lydia was three seats away from Sabrina, and her voice carried clearly to everyone nearby as she gossiped with the women around her.

'I cannot imagine why he brought *her* along with him,' she said, picking up her glass and drinking freely. 'I mean, that dress! You'd think she was going to a business meeting, not a *party*!'

'She obviously hasn't got a clue, Lydia,' Lucinda said loudly enough for everyone to hear. 'I mean, she doesn't look that young to me. You'd think she'd have learned *something* about what's expected.' She giggled. 'She's like a little dormouse, isn't she? I hope you've got plenty of cheese for her later!'

All those around her giggled loudly at that. Sabrina felt so totally overwhelmed at the position she was in now, she had difficulty not bursting into tears. She should never have come, never, never, never. And she'd never forgive Alexander for asking her.

Suddenly, unable to tolerate this for another moment, Alexander stood to his feet, pulling Sabrina up beside him. She glanced up quickly, her eyes moist with unshed tears.

He cleared his throat, looking around him. 'I think this is as good a moment as any to let everyone into our little secret—don't you, Sabrina?' he added, looking down at her.

'What secret? What are you on about, Alexander?' Lydia said shrilly.

'Well, for one thing, we can't stay for dinner with you after all,' he said.

'Not staying for dinner? Why ever not?' Lydia demanded.

Alexander waited a second, his eyes sending a dramatic signal to Sabrina as he squeezed her hand tightly.

'I'm afraid your…Sunday spectacular has coincided with a rather more important date in my life, *Lydia*,' he said. 'In fact, it's high time we were off.' He drew Sabrina closely to him. 'We have a rather *special* celebration of our own to attend, don't we, Sabrina?' he said.

Wide-eyed at this totally unexpected change of plan, but realizing that Alexander was looking for an excuse to leave, Sabrina returned his gaze calmly. She would respond in which ever way suited her boss, she thought.

'Of course,' she said. 'And I don't want to hurry you away, but I did make the booking for nine-thirty, and it's almost that now.' She paused. 'We mustn't be late,' she added.

Lydia was almost ready to explode with annoyance.

'What on earth is so important that you have to dash off?' she demanded.

Alexander hesitated just long enough to give his words full impact.

He glanced at his mother, and at the other women, a faint smile on the uncompromising mouth. 'Tonight, Sabrina and I are about to celebrate the fact that I have asked her not only to be my personal assistant, but to be my wife.' He looked down solemnly into the girl's wide-eyed, unbelieving gaze. 'And she has consented to do me that honour,' he added defiantly.

CHAPTER FOUR

WITH his arm closely across Sabrina's shoulders, Alexander guided her from the room and outside into the night. Neither of them said a word to each other as they walked rapidly towards the car, each fired up inside at what had just happened at the crowded dining-table.

Alexander could scarcely believe his mother's attitude and rudeness—but why was he so surprised? he asked himself. She'd never been one to consider the feelings of others, and older age was certainly not improving her in that respect.

As for Lucinda, and what she'd said, he shrugged inwardly. He didn't want to think about the woman at all. As far as he was concerned, she was a non-person, a nobody, a distant character from his past.

But Lydia could never be that distant; the blood tie was there, and couldn't be changed or ignored. He bit his lip. Even though he had made so many allowances for her behaviour when he was young, it still hurt Alexander to witness his mother's hurtful lack of concern for others. She wasn't an evil person, he thought helplessly—just impossibly egocentric.

They reached the car, and as he handed Sabrina into the passenger seat he could see that she was quietly furious with him. He raised one hand submissively, then closed the door and walked around to his side and got in, pausing for a moment before inserting the key into the ignition.

'Sorry,' he said briefly. 'It was the only thing I could come up with.'

'What? To get yourself out of the party you never wanted to come to anyway? Or were you hiding behind me to give your *lady friends* the final brush-off?' Sabrina clasped her hands together tightly, trying to regain control of her anger. It wasn't just anger she was feeling, it was acute anxiety. How on earth was this going to affect her job, her precious job? Could she possibly go on working with Alexander McDonald? Surely they'd both be horribly embarrassed in each other's company? Sabrina knew very well what she *should* do—she should give him her notice now! But did she have the strength of mind, could she afford, to walk away from that salary he was paying her?

Trying desperately hard to make some sense of this mind-boggling turn of events, she felt a surge of anger well up inside her. For his own ends, she thought, he had taken complete advantage of her, of her situation, saying the first stupid thing that had come into his head. She swallowed, keeping her voice deadly calm.

'Alexander,' she said quietly. 'I promised to be your secretary, your personal assistant, and to do everything in my power to help you with your present project. I did not expect to join you in a total and very public lie.'

'Yes. I thought you supported me very well,' he said. 'The booking you'd made for our dinner—what time did you say it was, nine-thirty?—sounded utterly convincing.' He paused and Sabrina saw his eyes twinkle maddeningly as she looked across at him. 'I'm beginning to feel quite hungry, actually,' he added.

Now he was teasing her, and this made Sabrina feel so annoyed she could have hit him.

'This isn't funny,' she said flatly. 'Because of who you are, our fictitious engagement is sure to get in the papers. What were you *thinking* of?'

He waited before replying. 'I was thinking of you,' he said quietly. 'And how you must be feeling. I was so incensed at my mother's behaviour that I decided to put the cat amongst the pigeons.' He looked across at Sabrina for a moment, thinking how unspoilt and defenceless she looked, and so appealing, even though she was clearly very angry with him. He shifted in his seat. 'And, by the way, I never hide behind anyone,' he said. 'If this does become public, we'll deny it, simple as that. It won't last more than one edition of any newspaper.' He put the key in the ignition and started the engine, glancing across at her again. 'And don't worry. You're quite safe with me. I don't intend marrying anyone—ever.'

Back at the party, with the deafening noise fuelled by drink louder than ever, Lydia looked around at the handful of her guests who'd been witness to Alexander's announcement. Determined not to let the staggering incident spoil the atmosphere, she said gaily, 'All that was total nonsense, of course! It'll never happen. My son is a writer. He's always making things up—makes his living at it!'

She paused, fixing each of them with an intensely steely gaze. 'And I do not expect a word of this to be breathed by anyone. Anyone at all.' She stared, almost glared, at the bewildered faces looking back at her. 'I hope I've made myself clear,' she added.

The four or five women concerned, looking back

fearfully at their majestic hostess, had no option but to agree that they'd all keep mum.

Sitting beside Alexander as he drove the car smoothly along the country roads, Sabrina began to calm down a bit. Although it had seemed a very impetuous thing for him to do, she couldn't help believing him when he said it had been his way of defending her feelings, of standing up for her. It certainly wasn't in his own interests to have said such a thing. Sabrina breathed a long, deep sigh and glanced across at him, at the chiselled features and strong chin, at the strength of his thighs clearly visible beneath the fine fabric of his trousers. She decided to offer an olive branch.

'I'm quite hungry too,' she said.

At once, the handsome face creased into a broad grin, and without looking at her he said, 'Wonderful. I know just the place.'

Twenty minutes later, still long before they'd reached the motorway, Alexander turned left into a narrow road. Half a mile along it they could see a sign which said 'The Woodcutter'. Almost immediately he pulled into a wooded car park and brought the car to a halt, glancing briefly across at Sabrina.

'I hope you're going to like this,' he said. 'I don't manage to get here very often, but it's certainly one of my favourite places to eat.'

Sabrina was still gazing up at the inviting-looking building, which she could see was almost completely surrounded by fir trees and holly bushes. The rosy lighting which shone from every latticed window added to its welcoming appearance.

'Well, at first glance this is a delightful place,' she

said. 'And rather remote. I didn't know it existed. How did you find it?'

He smiled at her, feeling upbeat and optimistic for a second—not only because he'd successfully extricated them both from his mother's party, but because he was here with Sabrina. He realized, with a jolt of surprise, how quickly she was melding into the fabric of his life. How, from almost the first day, she'd seemed to know exactly what was required of her without any fuss or unnecessary querying. Just his sort of woman, he thought, counting himself lucky that she'd accepted the post.

'Oh, I chanced upon it several years ago after visiting my parents,' he said in answer to her question. 'I haven't been here for a while, but the chef—if it's the same one—has a fine reputation.'

Sabrina waited for him to come round and open her door, thinking that whatever was on tonight's menu she'd enjoy it, because by now she was starving.

As they walked up the short path to the entrance, a comfortably happy sound of chatting and laughter reached their ears. Sabrina felt overwhelmingly thankful that she was here and not at Lydia's party. From nightmare to nirvana, she thought instinctively.

Almost at once, the man serving drinks at the crowded bar looked up and smiled, raising his hand in greeting.

'Hi, Alex!' he called over. 'Where've you been? Hiding yourself away again?'

Alexander moved towards the bar, his hand on Sabrina's waist for a second as he guided her slightly in front of him. 'Hello, Grant. Yes, sorry, I've been out of touch for a while.' He paused, noting the man's questioning glance in Sabrina's direction. 'I've brought my secretary, Sabrina, with me tonight for a well-deserved supper. Have you still got a table available?'

Grant nodded affably. He'd make sure he'd accommodate Alexander McDonald, his most famous customer. He finished pulling a pint for the man he was dealing with, then came from behind the bar to join Alexander and Sabrina. 'Sit over there by the window just for ten minutes, Alex,' he said. 'I'll send someone to take your drinks order, and a table will be available in the restaurant at nine-thirty. Is that OK?'

Sabrina and Alexander exchanged smiles, and he said, 'That suits us perfectly, doesn't it, Sabrina? Thanks, Grant.'

Sitting at their discreet table for two, Sabrina looked around her appreciatively, realizing just how much she'd missed this kind of occasion. As she looked up into the solemn gaze of Alexander's black eyes, studying her intently, she had to admit that she wasn't going to complain at being here. To be with such a handsome and attentive member of the opposite sex had a certain palpable magic, so she might as well enjoy it, she thought. Enjoy this evening which seemed to be turning into a theatrical production.

As the light from the candle flickering on the table in front of them lit up Sabrina's features, and her thoughts, Alexander sensed again that there was an unusual depth to her character—a depth which he'd like to delve into.

He suddenly remembered her telling him at the interview that she had a sister, so casually he enquired, 'How is your sister at the moment? I think you mentioned that she didn't enjoy the best of health.'

Brought back abruptly from her lingering thoughts, Sabrina put down her glass and looked across at him.

As her wide and moist eyes looked into his, Alexander had difficulty in not gently putting his fingers beneath her chin and tilting her face closer to his. Instead, he put down his own glass and waited for her to reply to his question.

'I sincerely hope that Melly is very well,' she said lightly. She paused. 'She flew to Spain this morning, on a teaching contract for a couple of weeks. I'm hoping that the complete change will do her good, cheer her up.' Sabrina sipped her drink. 'It's a music-and-dance school,' she explained. 'She's already texted to let me know they've arrived safely and are settling in.'

Alexander hadn't taken his eyes off her as she spoke. 'Melly is younger than you?' he asked, guessing that this was the case, because Sabrina's whole attitude told him that she obviously felt responsible for her sister.

'Only a couple of years,' Sabrina said. 'But she's sometimes rather vulnerable when life seems to get the better of her, and I do have to pick up some pieces occasionally.' She looked away for a moment. Melly was hundreds of miles away tonight, and must look after herself, but Sabrina was here sitting opposite the man who earlier this evening had taken it upon himself to inform anyone listening that she was about to become his wife! Another sudden wave of hot embarrassment swept over her as she remembered. That she was about to calmly eat supper with Alexander McDonald, and make inconsequential conversation with him, seemed absurd. She cleared her throat; she had to say something more about it, she thought.

'I know you made light of what happened at Lydia's party,' she said carefully. 'But I don't feel as convinced as you seem to be that no more will come of it.' She hesitated, lowering her voice. 'I still can't quite believe you said all that,' she added. 'I nearly dropped through the floor.'

'Well, you covered your discomfort very well,' he said smoothly. 'No one could have guessed that you weren't totally aware of—and happily in accordance with—the announcement.' He grinned suddenly, disarmingly. 'Forget it, Sabrina. It was an unexpected one-off, an unforeseen circumstance which we dealt with perfectly. And nothing has changed between us,' he said, leaning forward. 'You are my PA, and I am your somewhat demanding employer who expects you to rise to any occasion that may present itself. Which you did, with flying colours.' He sat back, as if that was the end of the matter. 'Ah, good, here comes our supper,' he said cheerfully.

To her surprise, Sabrina knew that she was going to be able to eat every morsel of the delicious food put in front of them, even though she admitted to feeling slightly traumatized at what had happened still. To hear herself discussed so publicly and so unpleasantly had been a horrible experience, and she knew she wouldn't forget it for a long time. Then, even worse, for Alexander to have announced that she'd accepted his proposal of marriage still left her feeling shattered. It was like a silly dream, the sort of thing which she and Melly sometimes told each other about as they chatted at breakfast time—though Melly's dreams were always more highly coloured than her own.

Sabrina shrugged inwardly. She and her boss would really have to forget that the wretched business had ever taken place, even though she knew, whatever he said, that she was going to feel awkward when she turned up for work tomorrow morning. How could she help it?

But now, as far as he was concerned, Alexander

seemed completely unfazed as he tucked into the rare steak he'd ordered. He glanced across at her.

'I thought you said you were hungry,' he said casually. 'You're not eating anything.'

Sabrina smiled quickly, then picked up her knife and fork. From the first mouthful her lamb cutlet and salad proved to be as mouth-watering as it looked.

'I was just thinking,' she said. 'That's all.'

'And apparently you can't eat and think at the same time?' he enquired, reaching for more mustard.

Sabrina didn't bother to answer that. Then she asked curiously, 'Why do you call your mother by her Christian name?'

Alexander didn't look up as he replied. 'Because that is what she told us to do when we were kids, my brother and I.' He picked up his glass of wine. 'Lydia never took kindly to motherhood, I'm afraid,' he went on, 'so as long as we didn't call her Mother—or, perish the thought, Mummy—she could forget she was one.' He looked thoughtful for a moment. 'Not long after I was born she got herself sterilized to avoid the fatal mistake of conceiving any more little brats.' His mouth twisted briefly. 'Makes you wonder why she bothered in the first place.'

Sabrina kept her eyes on her plate as she listened, her professional mind already forming familiar patterns. 'And your father—what about him?' she asked lightly, trying not sound as if she was interviewing a patient.

'Oh, no such hang-ups for Dad,' Alexander said. 'Even though Lydia wanted us to call him Angus. But he wouldn't hear of it, and we never did.'

'Was he at the party tonight?' Sabrina enquired innocently, realizing that she was developing an almost clinical interest in the McDonald family.

'Well, I didn't see him,' Alexander replied. 'But then, my mother's parties were never his thing. And as he works for an international bank he's seldom at home. Which gives him the perfect excuse,' Alexander added wryly.

By now, the good food, wine and enveloping warmth of the place were filling Sabrina with an overwhelming sense of contentment, so that everything that had happened earlier was actually beginning to slip comfortably into the background. Perhaps the news wouldn't get out and nothing would come of it, as Alexander had said, she thought. Then everyone, including herself, could forget the whole thing.

'You're thinking again,' Alexander accused her lightly. She smiled across at him now, the candlelight making her eyes more sparklingly green than ever as she trapped his gaze, holding him spellbound for a second.

'Sorry. I do rather a lot of it,' she said. 'Part of my training, I'm afraid.'

Suddenly, abruptly, he said, 'Is there a man in your life, Sabrina?'

The unexpectedness of the question almost threw her for a moment, then she smiled crookedly.

'Not any more,' she said quietly.

There was a long pause, during which neither of them spoke.

'Stephen—my fiancé—was killed in a tragic, bizarre accident eighteen months ago.'

'I'm sorry.'

Sabrina shrugged briefly. 'Time passes. One has to accept what life throws at you.' She drained her glass. 'I don't expect ever to marry now,' she went on casually. 'For one thing, my sister comes first. And for another...' Sabrina looked wistful as she looked across at Alexander. 'I don't intend placing myself at the mercy of fate a second time. It's just not worth the risk. Or the agony.'

Much later, after he'd dropped Sabrina back home, Alexander sat in his study, his legs propped up on the desk, and stared pensively into his glass of whisky. That had been quite an evening, he thought, and it hadn't turned out as badly as he might have expected.

To his own enormous surprise, he realized that he had really enjoyed being off-duty with Sabrina Gold, that he had not wanted the evening to end. His new secretary didn't fall into the normal category of womankind he'd been used to—all of whom had very quickly bored him to death. Which was probably all his own fault, he reasoned. So, what? What was bugging him like this at gone one o'clock in the morning? He frowned briefly as his thoughts ran on. Why would such a young, beautiful woman declare herself out of bounds for the rest of her life? Why was she so negative about her possible future?

He drained his glass, then swung his legs from the desk and stood up. What the hell was it to him, anyway? he asked himself. His mouth twisted. At least there was one good thing about it—with no man on the scene, there wouldn't be any occasional stupid, romantic emotional problems to deal with, to hold things up here. His work was the only important thing to be considered.

He stared down at the shadowy garden below, at the street lights casting their gentle beams across the grass, then turned abruptly and strode from the room.

Alexander McDonald knew exactly what was getting to him. For some reason, he was suddenly feeling emotionally out of his depth where his secretary was concerned. But why? Well, he'd soon put that right, he thought irritably. Tomorrow morning it would be Cinderella time—business as usual!

CHAPTER FIVE

AMAZINGLY, Sabrina managed to feel fairly normal when she arrived for work the next morning, even though she'd found it very difficult to get any sleep.

Once again, Maria was just leaving the house, and the two women smiled at each other.

'Hullo, dear,' Maria said. 'My, you do look smart. What an unusual-colour top you've got on: what do you call that?'

'I think it's taupe,' Sabrina replied, thinking that she didn't feel very smart this morning. She'd woken late and grabbed the first thing that had come to hand in her wardrobe. But she was glad of the compliment.

'I'll just pop along to the shop and get Mr McDonald his newspapers,' Maria said as she went past. 'I'll leave them all in the kitchen, as usual. He's already working in the study,' she added over her shoulder.

The mere mention of newspapers made Sabrina's tongue go dry; there couldn't possibly be anything in them about Alexander yet, surely?

She tapped lightly on the door of the study before going in. Alexander looked up, angry at the rush of pleasure he felt at seeing her again, especially as he'd given himself a good talking-to last night before he'd eventually got to sleep. His unusual interest in his new secretary was totally unexpected, totally unlike him, and if he wasn't careful it was going to intrude on his work plans. He was not interested in Sabrina Gold's past life and loves or her future, he told himself. The only thing which concerned him was the present and her presence here as his personal assistant.

'I'd like all this typed up ASAP—and then I want to hear you read it out,' he said, deliberately keeping his tone formal. He sighed. 'I think I'm getting there, at last, and not before time,' he added, handing Sabrina a thick sheaf of papers.

Sabrina couldn't help smiling inwardly. As he had said would be the case, today and from now on it would be business as usual. She was his secretary and he was the boss. Could it only have been a handful of hours ago that they'd sat opposite each other, drinking wine, letting their hair down, telling each other things?

She avoided looking at him again, immediately setting to work, and before long she found herself engrossed in the writing she was typing out. He was an outstanding author; she really must find time to read one of his books for herself. Even from the fragmented chapters she'd so far seen, she'd felt completely immersed in the lives of his complex characters. No wonder he sometimes looked as if he was in another world, she thought.

It was almost twelve before Sabrina was satisfied that she'd got everything typed up accurately before printing it out. She stretched back, raising her arms above her head and flexing her tense shoulder muscles. She and her boss had not exchanged a word for almost three hours, and had not even been disturbed by the phone ringing for once. Sabrina realized, with a slight pang of guilt, that she hadn't made them any coffee yet, either.

She glanced across at Alexander who was sitting with

his back to her, staring thoughtfully up at the ceiling. She cleared her throat.

'Sorry; I've been so engrossed, I forgot all about our coffee.'

He turned his head slowly to look at her. 'That isn't important,' he said. 'Anyway, isn't it nearly time we thought about something for our lunch?'

Suddenly the telephone rang, and Sabrina automatically reached out to answer it, colour flooding her cheeks as Lydia's familiar voice reached her ears.

'Hello? This is Lydia. Is that you, Alexander? I have been trying all morning to reach you on your mobile, but you seem to have switched it off.'

'Um, just a second; I'll see if Mr McDonald is available,' Sabrina said faintly, trying not to sound panicky. 'It's Lydia,' she mouthed to Alexander.

He raised his eyes briefly, but picked up his extension.

'Good morning, Lydia,' he said casually.

'Why on earth aren't you using your mobile, Alexander? I do not expect to have to ring the office in order to speak to my son.'

'There are certain points in my working life, Lydia, when I need to be unavailable—to all-comers.' He paused. 'Anyway, how can I help? There's nothing wrong, I hope?'

'Of course there's nothing wrong. Not with me, anyway!' Lydia sighed heavily. 'I really rang to find out how *you* were this morning. It was strange that you went home so early last night. I hardly had time to speak to you at all.' There was a moment's pause. 'I suppose you had to get back to your writing.'

Alexander smiled slowly to himself, catching Sabrina's eye for a second. This was obviously a fishing phone-call, he thought, for his mother to find things out. Of course, he knew that his mother was not going to sully her lips by referring to the engagement announcement. She was certainly not going to bring his secretary into the conversation, nor to even mention her by name. It was obvious that Lydia was going to pretend that the incident had never taken place—so he would play her game, which would be convenient for all concerned.

'Oh, my work is always *much* more important to me than socializing, Lydia. You know that,' he said. 'And, as a matter of fact, I have exactly four weeks to meet the deadline for my current novel and I still haven't completed the penultimate chapter. So, as you can imagine, my time is precious.'

There was more silence as Lydia battled with her thoughts. Then she said, 'Well, just so long as you're feeling OK, Alexander. I did wonder, you know, last night, whether you may have been overdoing things a bit—losing your grip on reality,' she added through pursed lips.

Alexander couldn't help a slow smile creasing his mouth. 'Whatever would give you that idea, Lydia?' he said. 'No, I assure you that I'm perfectly well and in full possession of all my faculties. You really mustn't worry about me.'

He could almost see his mother shake her head in total perplexity, and he was enjoying every moment of her confusion.

'So, if there's nothing else, Lydia, I must fly.' He shuffled some papers and yawned volubly. 'And now my lovely secretary is about to make me a nice sandwich for my lunch before a meeting with my editor later this afternoon.'

They ended the call, and he looked across at Sabrina.

'You no doubt got the gist of all that, I'm sure?' he said casually. He paused. 'My mother has always been very good at sweeping anything which she doesn't like under the carpet.' He stood up. 'That is why she deliberately did not mention our *exciting* news.' He grinned suddenly. 'I'm sure she was hoping for some further information on the matter—hopefully a denial or, heaven help her, a confirmation. And I had the greatest pleasure in not providing either.'

He looked at Sabrina solemnly. 'So there you have it, Sabrina. Least said, soonest mended. You can forget the whole thing.'

Sabrina looked at him doubtfully. 'But what about Lucinda...and the others?'

Alexander walked over to the door. 'Oh, I'm quite certain my mother would have given them all precise instructions to keep their mouths shut... Anyway, by the end of yesterday evening, they would all have been very much the worse for wear. Probably don't remember anything at all today.'

Although Sabrina wasn't entirely convinced at that, she realized that Alexander was probably right. He clearly understood his mother and her friends very well. In any case, perhaps what had happened last night wasn't all that unusual. Maybe he had done this kind of thing before—after all, she knew nothing about the details of his personal life and loves. He might have had many fleeting relationships that no one took seriously, that came to nothing.

She followed him as they went downstairs into the kitchen. As usual, Maria had brought plenty of food in, and soon Sabrina was filling fresh slices of bread with succulent ham and some grated cheese while Alexander made their coffee.

Presently, sitting side by side on the tall stools by the kitchen bar, he glanced across at her.

'I've told you all about my parents,' he said between mouthfuls. 'What about yours? Are they still…?'

'Oh, Philippa, my mother, moved to Australia over ten years ago with her new husband,' Sabrina said. 'My father walked out on us when I was seven. I hardly remember what he looked like,' she added casually. 'My sister was only five then, and as my mother had to go out to work to support us it fell to me to look after the house, always to be there to take care of Melly.' Sabrina paused, picking up her mug of coffee. 'Anyway, some years later—I was sixteen—my mother met David, an Australian. After a whirlwind affair they married and went to live in Sydney.' She sipped from her mug. 'We hear from them. Occasionally,' she added.

There was silence for a few seconds. 'I imagine you had to grow up pretty quickly, Sabrina, having to take responsibility for your sister from such a young age after your father abandoned his family.'

Sabrina smiled quickly. 'I never really thought about it like that,' she said. 'But, yes, I suppose I did grow up almost overnight. Anyway.' She nibbled at her sandwich. 'Melly and I were always close, even as small kids—it sort of came naturally to me to take care of her,' she added.

'Do you go to Australia much to see your mother?' Alexander wanted to know.

'We've been twice,' Sabrina said. She hesitated. 'Time and distance eventually alienates you even from close relations,' she said simply. 'My mother has a new life, new friends. She can well do without us hindering her plans.' Sabrina's mouth twisted briefly. 'I got the distinct impression that she was relieved to wave us off back home last time.'

Alexander looked solemn for a moment, an unexpected rush of compassion filling him as he considered what Sabrina had just told him. She hadn't exactly had an easy life, he thought, yet she'd never demonstrated even a hint of self-pity in her attitude—except, perhaps, when she'd spoken about her fiancé last night. No, not self-pity, he amended, just sadness—genuine sadness.

Suddenly Sabrina smiled brightly. 'But the good news is that my sister seems to be on cloud nine at the moment. We had a long, long phone-call early today, and all the signs are very positive. The people she's with are very friendly and helpful, and she loves the place they're staying in. In fact, she sounded happier than she's been for a long time. Apparently work starts in earnest tomorrow, and she can't wait!'

'That must be a real relief for you,' Alexander said, feeling glad for Sabrina's sake. Well, anyone would feel sympathy for another human being who'd had more than her fair share of life's custard pies, he thought. He couldn't help comparing Sabrina's lot with his own and his brother's. Although Lydia had always been a non-parent, he and Bruno had never wanted for any material thing, had never known hardship of any kind. Angus was a loyal and affectionate father, even though he was so often away from the UK. And there had always been others on hand to supply their every need.

But what of his relationship with *his* sibling? Alexander asked himself. The two boys had always been grimly competitive, that was a well-known fact. It was fortunate that the famous brothers had each been so highly successful in their different careers. But they certainly did not enjoy the warmth and closeness that

Sabrina and her sister so obviously did, and for the first time in his life Alexander felt regretful about that. He stared out of the window for a second as he finished the last of his coffee. It must be good, it must be brilliant, to be so deeply loved by anyone, he thought. Loved selflessly, with no regrets and with no expectation of anything in return. Just love for its own sake.

Sabrina got down from her stool and turned to Alexander. 'More coffee?' she asked, and he shook his head.

'No thanks, I'm fine for now.' He glanced at his watch. 'I'll go and pick up the printout you did this morning and take it with me to the editor. I'm due in town shortly.' He paused. 'There's all the scribbles I did earlier relating to my final chapter for you to decipher, Sabrina,' he said, and paused. 'I should be back by five-thirty, but if I'm going to be delayed I'll give you a ring.'

'Fine,' Sabrina said as she drew water into the sink to wash up their things, privately making up her mind that with Alexander safely out of the way she would find time to clean up the study a bit. Working amongst dust and disorder put her teeth on edge. She'd already spotted where Maria kept all the dusters and polish.

As Alexander was about to leave the room, his mobile rang and he glanced over at Sabrina as he clicked it on. 'I knew this morning had been just too peaceful,' he said. 'Hi, Bruno!'

It suddenly struck Sabrina as weird that she was finding herself caught up in the lives of the famous McDonald brothers. As she glanced briefly over at Alexander, she saw him make a face.

'I'm honestly too caught up here with my own stuff to offer you any time, Bruno,' he began, then stopped as Bruno interrupted. After a couple of minutes he said, 'Oh, OK, then. Look, why don't you send the script over for me to have a look at first, then perhaps we could have a bite out somewhere on Sunday at lunch time.' He paused. 'We haven't got together for a long time, Bruno. It'll be a chance to put that right.' Even as he spoke, Alexander was surprised at his own suggestion, but knew that Sabrina's influence had something to do with it. Perhaps he and Bruno should make time to see each other now and then. Neither of them made any effort in that direction, he thought, but it was never too late to change things.

There was another pause as he listened to his brother again. 'OK, fine. And if I'm not here my secretary will be, and you can give it to her. What? No, no, it's not Janet. She's retired and I've got a new PA now. Sabrina. Yes, Sabrina! And yes, yes…' Sabrina saw Alexander make another face. 'Yes, Bruno, have no fear of that… And she's competent as well,' he said flatly.

The call ended and Alexander glanced back at Sabrina as he went towards the door. 'Someone will be calling by to drop an envelope in at some point—could be this week, it could be next,' he said. 'Anyway, see you later,' he added briefly as he left the room.

That was the trouble with Bruno, Alexander thought irritably as he went up the stairs. He only ever thought of women in terms of their sex appeal. His brother had immediately wanted to know what Sabrina looked like, whether she had a good figure…. Alexander had far too much respect, especially since Sabrina had been listening!

As he went into his bathroom for a quick wash and brush-up, he looked thoughtfully at himself in the mirror for a second. How *would* he describe Sabrina to someone

who'd never met her? he thought. Well, there was no difficulty there. She was small, with small hands and feet
and a heart-shaped face, a slightly tip-tilted nose and
desirable, full lips; she had long, fair hair almost down
to her waist but always immaculately groomed. But the
colour of those eyes, those magical eyes... They were
a translucent green, like the deepest part of a placid
ocean.

But... She wore no make-up, no nail varnish, no
heady, sickening perfume; no pretence of any kind.

Not Bruno's type at all, Alexander thought with some
satisfaction.

Later, armed with a floor cloth, disinfectant, polish
and some dusters, Sabrina went upstairs to the study.
Through the partly open door of a large cupboard along
the landing, she'd seen a vacuum cleaner and brushes.
Good; that should all be quite sufficient to sort out
Alexander McDonald's mess, she thought.

The first thing she did was to open all the windows
in the study and let in some fresh air. Then, turning, she
went across to the *chaise longue*, filled her arms with
all the cushions and went over to bang them furiously
together out through the window. The dust flew out
in clouds, causing her to sneeze three times in quick
succession. That hadn't been done in a long time, she
thought—but no blame could be attached to Maria, who
wasn't even allowed in this room.

A sudden thought struck Sabrina for a moment and
she went over to the small pile of dusters, selecting one
which had obviously not been used, because it was still
neatly folded, and tied it around her head. At least that
would be some protection.

Then she started to tackle the floor. Masses of dust

had gathered along the skirting boards and in the corners; picking up a broom, she began sweeping it up carefully, collecting it in the dustpan she'd found. The vacuum cleaner could do the rest, she thought, going over to switch it on.

As she moved the machine briskly over the huge Persian rug, she soon began to see the colourful design beneath. Although it clearly wasn't new, it was a beautiful piece of soft furnishing which must have cost a fortune. When she'd finished that, she got down on her hands and knees and polished the dark-oak flooring until it shone, realizing that she was actually enjoying doing all this. She'd never minded house work in any case, but doing it in someone else's place was slightly more interesting, or so it seemed just then. When she was satisfied that the whole area resembled something other than a receptacle for grime, Sabrina stood back and surveyed it critically. Well, that would do for a start.

But there was still a long way to go, and for the next two hours she took down and wiped clean all the books from the shelves, polished the oak doors of the fitted cupboards and worked a damp sponge along the window frames.

She decided to leave Alexander's desk until last. Then she suddenly realized that there was still the old granite fireplace to deal with, almost hidden by a couple of high-backed chairs standing in front of it. With almost wild abandon, she scooped up all the bric-a-brac from the mantelpiece: old post cards, a torch which didn't work, a box of matches, a nail file, a cork screw, a box of tissues, another one of plasters and some cough sweets. She shook her head as she put it all to one side. *How can anyone—how can Alexander McDonald—live like this?* she thought. But then, he didn't live here, this was where he worked. And none of this disorder registered with him. He only had eyes for the words taking form in front of him.

Standing in front of the chimneypiece was a huge jug of dried flowers long past their sell-by date, so that they had mostly disintegrated into a powdery heap. Well, she'd dump those and replace them with some fresh greenery from the garden. She'd spotted plenty of bushes down there that had some colourful leaves on one or two of them.

When she finally got round to tidying his desk, Sabrina realized that here she must not take liberties. This was Alexander's domain, and he wouldn't like anything put back differently.

Sitting herself in his chair for a moment, it gave Sabrina a genuine thrill as she stared at everything in front of her. There were countless pens, pencils—most of them chewed at the top—rubbers, sticking tape, directories and reference books. Not many people had the chance to sit here where all the imagination flowed, all the expertise, culminating in Alexander's books, which sold in their millions. Almost reverentially, Sabrina cleaned the dust from every corner of the desk, wiped over the computer and telephone and tidied the books, before replacing everything she'd moved back to where it had been before.

Suddenly, a small snapshot fell to the floor; it had obviously been tucked inside a page somewhere. Picking it up, Sabrina saw that it was a picture of a somewhat younger Alexander on a beach somewhere, tanned and wearing a brief pair of swimming trunks, his arms clasped tightly around the waist of a dark-haired young woman in a bikini. She was gazing up at him adoringly, and the whole scene told its own story. Those were two people very much in love.

Sabrina put the snap back into one of the books, wondering who that girl had been. Someone who was once very special to Alexander, she thought.

Then she shrugged. There were no doubt plenty of other photographs like that, of other women in his life—why did it bother her? And of course it didn't, not a bit.

Decisively, Sabrina finished what she was doing before putting away all the cleaning stuff she'd been using. Then, letting herself out of the back entrance, she slipped outside into the garden to pick an armful of foliage to put in the jug. It cheered that black grate up no end. Looking around at her afternoon's handiwork, she felt satisfyingly gratified. The whole room looked pleasant now, almost habitable.

Glancing at her watch, Sabrina saw that it was already five-thirty—and she hadn't done a scrap of that typing he'd left for her! *Help!* He would be back soon, because he hadn't rung to say he was delayed.

Suddenly feeling quite exhausted, Sabrina moved over to the *chaise longue* and without thinking collapsed down on to it, lying down and resting her head back, closing her eyes. Just for a few moments, she thought. Just a few moments to recover.

Alexander looked down at the sleeping form of his secretary, a strange expression on his face. His gaze swept around the room, taking in the shining floorboards, the amazingly bright rug, the books on his shelves standing to attention, the smell of polish and fresh air and the casually elegant display of greenery in the fireplace. A slow smile touched his lips as he stood, motionless, for a few moments. Well, she'd asked permission to clean up and he'd agreed. He had to admit that an unusual sense of well-being came over him as he looked around. It was a very pleasant experience to see his study—which sometimes felt like his prison—so *cared-for.*

Then his eyes softened as he looked back at Sabrina. Even with a bright-yellow duster tied around her head and a dark smudge of dust on her nose, she looked, well, wonderful, he thought. Wonderful, vulnerable... He turned abruptly to leave the room just as her eyes flickered open, and she struggled to sit up.

'Heavens! What's the time?' she faltered, looking up at him. 'I only meant to sit down for a moment. I must have dozed off...'

'Well, from what I can see all around me, I'm not surprised,' Alexander said, reaching his hand out to raise her up. 'It's six. It took me a bit longer to get back, I'm afraid.' He paused. 'Sabrina, you've transformed the study. Thank you—thank you very much.'

She smiled up at him. 'I quite enjoyed doing it, but I haven't done any of the rather more important work you left for me, Alexander...'

He placed his hand briefly on her shoulder. 'There's always tomorrow,' he said. 'And now I'm going to take you home. You've had a long, long day.'

CHAPTER SIX

ON THURSDAY, two weeks later, Sabrina was feeling so involved with Alexander McDonald's work and lifestyle, she felt she'd known him for ever. They seemed to have developed a rapport so quickly that any dread she might have felt about working for such an important man—who'd left her in no doubt at the interview that a lot would be expected of her—had disappeared almost overnight. But she did concede that her own qualifications had been an advantage because she had learned to read his mindset straight away, and knew when it was wise to say something or when to keep quiet. And she took it as a great compliment that he sometimes asked her opinion about something he was agonizing over as he wrote. She realized, with some surprise, that even great writers seemed to need constant reassurance and encouragement. The fact that he ran something by her occasionally made her feel ridiculously proud.

To her relief, the penultimate chapter of his current novel had been approved, and now they were well into the final moments, the denouement of the story. How on earth was he going to bring it all together? she asked herself.

As she typed up the first draft of the last chapter, she felt herself completely caught up with the plot, as if this total fiction of his mattered, really mattered. She would buy his books from now on, she decided, all of them. Because now she had an intensely personal interest in anything and everything that concerned Alexander McDonald.

Of course by now his dreadful scrawl had become as plain as day to Sabrina. What she'd found so difficult to make out on that first day was not difficult any more. He seemed amazed at how quickly she was able to pass him the most recent printout.

Sabrina's present feeling of being so upbeat had a lot to do with Melly's experience in Spain. They'd only had three phone conversations since she had left, and each one had been full of how well everything was going over there; how Melly was being complimented on her work and attitude; how much fun she was having. Sabrina could barely recognize the voice at the other end. Her sister was usually the one whose pint was always half-empty rather than half-full, but there was no hint of pessimism now. She was having a ball, and although Sabrina was careful not to mention anything about health it was quite obvious that her sister was feeling on top of the world, with no talk of her being depressed or anxious about anything at all. A hasty text this week had informed Sabrina that the tour had been extended, possibly for two or three weeks.

At around midday the front-door bell rang and Sabrina stopped typing and looked up in surprise. They seldom, if ever, had any visitors.

Going downstairs, she opened the door to see the instantly recognizable figure of Bruno McDonald standing there, casually dressed in black trousers and blue rugby-shirt. He was tall and broad-shouldered, and although there was an obvious likeness to his brother it was clear at Sabrina's first glance that it was Alexander who'd been especially endowed by nature. For one thing, Bruno did not possess the same spectacular jet-black eyes, the same magnetic, searching expression…

His smile was friendly, and more than interested in Sabrina as he looked down at her.

'Ah, you must be the new secretary—the lovely Sabrina,' he drawled lazily, his glance sweeping from Sabrina's face, down the entire length of her body and back again, making her feel as if she was standing there with nothing on.

'Yes, I'm Sabrina, Mr McDonald,' she said hesitantly. 'I'm afraid your brother is not here at the moment. He goes to the gym on Thursdays.'

Bruno waited a second before answering. 'Yes, I know, and I realized he probably wouldn't be back yet. But I was in the area and thought it worth dropping in. I want to talk to him about something he's looking at for me.' He smiled slowly. 'I'll come in and wait for him.'

Sabrina stood back at once for him to come inside. 'Of course. Can I make you a coffee?'

'That would be most kind, Sabrina.' The words which anyone might use, but spoken in that particular way, made Sabrina feel distinctly uncomfortable. She hoped Alexander wouldn't be long.

Bruno followed her along the hall into the kitchen, and presently stood idly leaning against the wall, his hands in his pockets, watching Sabrina as she filled the kettle.

'So, how long has…Sabrina been working for my brother?' he enquired.

'Oh, just a few weeks,' Sabrina replied, not looking at him, not wanting to make eye contact.

'Well, now, and what's he like as an employer?'

Bruno said. 'Of course, the other woman—Janet—was with him for absolutely ages, put up with him for years, so I suppose she was used to his ways. But—' he paused '—I imagine that Alexander can be difficult—a bit of a brute at times.'

Now Sabrina turned and looked at Bruno squarely. 'On the contrary,' she said coolly, 'I have never found Mr McDonald to be anything other than entirely businesslike and professional.'

How dreadful was this? she thought. Discussing Alexander under his own roof with a complete stranger, even if it was with a member of the family. She was beginning to heartily dislike the man standing there beside her. If his manner and approach were anything to go by he couldn't be less like Alexander. Even at the very beginning Sabrina had always felt relaxed and comfortable with her boss, which was not how she was feeling at the moment.

'Well, well, perhaps you're a good influence on him,' Bruno said languidly. 'Maybe a fresh face…and a fresh figure…was what he'd needed all along,' he added with heavy emphasis.

By now, Sabrina's nerve endings were really beginning to tingle. Any minute, Bruno McDonald was going to make a pass at her, she thought.

As she busied herself with preparing his drink, she turned and glanced back at him, changing the subject.

'I think we're having what they call an "Indian summer",' she said casually. 'For October it's really warm today, isn't it?'

'It certainly is,' he agreed. 'And I, personally, *love* warm weather because it encourages all you lovely girlies to dress in your scantiest, most revealing clothes.' He paused, deliberately staring at Sabrina again; she cringed, wishing that she'd not chosen to wear her rather low-cut top this morning. But it was the coolest one she owned, and it was sometimes rather hot working upstairs in the study.

'Of course, in winter,' he went on, 'you all insist on covering yourselves up in layers and layers of thick things. Which is such a shame for all us susceptible males lusting in the wings for a glimpse or two of the female form.'

If he doesn't shut up, Sabrina thought, irritated, *I'm going to tell him where to go.*

She was moving across to the cupboard where they kept the biscuits, standing on tiptoe to reach the tin, when Bruno immediately came up behind her. With one hand on her shoulder, he leaned across her and took the biscuits down from the shelf. With his face close to Sabrina's now, he looked down at her solemnly, and she could smell alcohol on his heavy breath.

'Now, Sabrina, if you had eaten up all your greens when you were a little girl, you would have grown a bit taller,' he said reprovingly.

Then, unbelievably, he slipped his hand from her shoulder and cupped it deliberately over her breast, squeezing it gently for a second. To which Sabrina's immediate response was to dig her elbow hard into the most vulnerable part of his solar plexus so that he staggered back, only just managing to stifle a painful, 'Ouch!'

For a few moments, Sabrina stood and glared at him, her eyes like jewelled daggers ready to strike, when thankfully the door opened and Alexander stood there. He looked first at Sabrina, then at Bruno, then back at Sabrina—and he could see straight away that something wasn't right. The atmosphere was undeniably charged, and he'd never seen an expression on Sabrina's face like that before.

Standing there in his shorts and T-shirt, his hair damp and tousled, he said, 'What's going on, Sabrina?'

'Oh, it's all right…it's nothing, really,' she began, her voice clearly unsteady.

But that tremulous remark of hers only confirmed Alexander's understanding of the situation, and for a dramatic moment he had difficulty in not punching his brother squarely between the eyes. *Bloody Bruno!*

'Alex, dear boy!' Bruno said, totally unfazed by his brother's arrival, or indeed by the thunderous look on his face. 'I thought I'd chance my luck that you might be able to see me for half an hour,' he said. He looked back at Sabrina. 'Your delightful secretary is just making me a coffee, which is sweet of her.'

But Alexander McDonald was nobody's fool, and he knew his brother. He went over to stand between Bruno and Sabrina. Putting his arm lightly on her shoulder, he could feel her shaking. 'Get out, Bruno,' Alexander said in a way that brooked no argument. 'I'm busy.'

'Oh, but I was hoping to show you this latest thing I'm interested in,' Bruno began. 'Hoping for your…input, Alex.'

'I repeat—get out,' Alexander said, keeping his voice calm with great difficulty. 'And please do not expect to just drop in any old time without letting me know first,' he added.

For the next few moments, Sabrina really thought she was going to faint. Where had she landed *this* time? Although she could see that Alexander guessed that his brother had behaved inappropriately, just how was this going to affect her chances now, her position here? Might Bruno McDonald even accuse her of leading him on, if Alexander demanded an explanation? She shuddered as she recalled his podgy hand mauling her.

But, feeling Alexander's protective grip on her shoulder, Sabrina knew that he had assessed the situation straight away, and she began to relax a bit. For her part, she would never tell her boss exactly what had upset her just now, she thought. In any case, it had hardly been the most mind-shattering thing to have taken place. But, still, it had taken her completely unawares and all she wished now was that she was out of here and safely back at home.

Alexander strode across the room and opened the door wide. 'Allow me to show you out, Bruno,' he said bluntly. 'And I repeat—next time, have the courtesy to inform me that you're going to call in. It's the least anyone should expect,' he added.

Bruno raised his arms helplessly, as if he didn't know why he was suddenly so unwelcome in his brother's house. 'Oh, deary me,' he said laconically. 'I have obviously hit a nerve or two this morning, haven't I?' He looked across at Sabrina whose cheeks had gone from rosy to almost deathly pale in the last few moments. 'You must understand, Sabrina, that we creative types can be difficult, prone to moodiness from time to time, and today is clearly one of those times. My brother doesn't seem to be a very happy boy, does he?'

Bruno sauntered over to leave the room, glancing back for a second. 'I wish you the best of luck, my dear,' he added. 'Enjoy the rest of your day.'

Then he was gone, and presently Alexander came back into the kitchen and looked down at Sabrina, who was still rooted to the spot.

'I...I won't ask you to elaborate, Sabrina,' he said quietly. 'All I will do is to apologize, profusely, for any inconvenience my brother put you to while I was out. Because clearly he had.'

Sabrina managed to smile faintly. 'I don't want to say anything about it, Alexander—as I said, it was nothing…not really. It was just a silly man behaving like silly men do. It's not the first time I've experienced it, and it won't be the last. Unfortunately,' she added.

But not from Alexander, Sabrina thought; never from him. Despite Bruno's ridiculous parting-shot, she had always felt comfortable, secure and totally at ease alone with her boss. How could two brothers be so unalike? Perhaps the touchy-feely theatrical world was to blame, she thought, glad that Melly had never been exposed to Bruno's sickening advances for more than a few moments at those auditions she'd attended. If she herself was ever put in that position with the man again, she thought savagely, she'd find an even more tender part of his anatomy to make her point.

'Well, anyway,' Alexander said, still clearly ruffled. 'Let's not ruin the rest of our day by thinking about my brother any further.' He paused. 'Do you feel like making us a sandwich while I pop up and have a quick shower? We've an afternoon's work ahead of us.'

'Wilco,' she said, touching her forehead in a mock salute.

As she prepared some toasted sandwiches for their lunch, Sabrina's thoughts centred on Melly for a moment. It seemed such a long time since her sister had left for Spain—and the girl didn't seem in any particular hurry to return! Although Sabrina was missing her a lot, she admitted to feeling carefree for the first time in ages. *Well, I'd better enjoy it*, she thought, *because when Melly returns nothing much will really have changed*

*and there'll be the inevitable sense of anti-climax to
deal with.*

But she mustn't think of all that now, she thought. She
was looking forward to this afternoon, when she'd be
reading aloud all the stuff she'd typed so far in this final
chapter of Alexander's novel. Knowing all his characters
by now, she felt she knew exactly how it should sound.
How she would make it sound, bring it all to life.

Soon, now wearing dark, well-cut trousers and a fine,
light-grey shirt, Alexander sat in his chair facing away
from Sabrina, staring out of the window as she settled
down to read the printout.

Keeping her voice firm and modulated, Sabrina
began to feel something like an electric thrill cours-
ing down her spine. This wasn't work, this was total,
utter pleasure, she thought gratefully. As the simple yet
masterful prose began to take shape as it was spoken
aloud, Sabrina felt honoured again to be the first one,
apart from the author, to hear it. It was like marking out
the first footsteps on an expanse of freshly fallen snow.
It was a privilege.

Alexander listened intently. She knew he wouldn't
interrupt her, but once or twice she was aware of him
bending his head to write something briefly on the pad
on his knee.

So intensely did Sabrina feel her emotions being
stirred as the story developed that, as she came to a
particularly poignant section in which the two main
protagonists were having a terrible, violent quarrel, her
voice rose and fell in anguish at the impossible situation they were in. Why would people say such dreadful
things to each other? she thought, her own thoughts
silently interrupting the plot. How could anyone be so

vicious? And further on, when it seemed unlikely that anything could ever be resolved, she felt such a degree of helplessness that her voice actually broke as she read out the plaintive dialogue, the longing in the sentiments expressed. It was magical writing, leaving her almost breathless.

It took more than half an hour for Sabrina to get to the end, and when she'd finished she stayed quite still, looking down at the script, not wanting to break the spell which Alexander McDonald had put her under. That long, last passage had been so full of heat, of passion, that she felt physically exhausted. And when she finally looked up Alexander had swivelled his chair around and was gazing down at her, a strange expression on his face.

'Thank you, Sabrina,' he said quietly, his eyes almost melting as he saw a large tear slip down Sabrina's cheek. She was such a sensitive woman, he thought, so readily in tune with what she'd been reading.

There was a long pause. 'I just wish that everyone who read my books—read any writer's books—would take the time to engage as you've just done,' he said. 'So many people skim-read, don't give true value to all the blood, sweat and tears which go into fiction. But you, Sabrina—you just brought all that alive, even to me, who knew what was coming!' He smiled. 'In fact, I learned something fresh about my characters and their motives just listening to you.' He hesitated. 'Have you—have you ever done stage work…any acting?' he asked.

Sabrina shook her head, suddenly feeling embarrassed that she'd had difficulty restraining her tears, knowing that he'd seen them. 'No, that's not my thing,' she said, wiping her nose with a tissue. 'That's my sister's domain.'

Alexander cleared his throat. 'One or two small points did strike me which I'd like us to discuss.'

He identified the parts he was referring to, and for the next hour they picked over his doubts together, tossing ideas back and forth between them. Sabrina could never have dreamed in a million years that she'd ever be asked to do such a thing. Alexander seemed to take on board every suggestion she plucked up the courage to make.

Finally, Sabrina stood up. 'I'm in need of a strong cup of tea, Alexander.'

'I think we could both do with a break,' he said. 'That was quite a marathon. But useful, very useful.'

After she had gone downstairs, Alexander sat staring into space for a while, still hearing Sabrina's sweet voice lingering in his ears. He admitted to a feeling of disquiet suddenly, because he realized that his new secretary was making herself so indispensable to him it would be an almost impossible task ever to do without her. But one day he would have to; he knew that. With her qualifications, it was obvious that she would want to return to her own profession at some point, and he would never try to dissuade her. That would be unfair; wrong. It wasn't just the fact that her work was so neat and meticulous, it was everything else which any employer yearned for in an employee—an attitude, a readiness to comply, to take the rough with the smooth, to be flexible and still keep a smile on her face.

He sighed heavily. The thought that one day she wouldn't be sitting there in his study filled him with an acute depression. Depression, something that hit him from time to time, had been blissfully absent since he'd taken her on. Then he squared his shoulders. For heaven's sake, she hadn't resigned—not yet—and it could be well into next year before the economic situation improved and she was offered her job back. Until then, she was his. He was paying good money—and he'd pay more if necessary to keep her by his side.

Later, as they sipped their tea in comparative silence, each with their own thoughts, Alexander said, 'I think it's time to call it a day, now, Sabrina. We're both tired.'

He looked down at her, for the first time noticing how some loose fronds of her hair had escaped from the band she was wearing and were falling prettily either side of her face and across her forehead. It made her look childlike and, to him, utterly adorable. He wished he had the courage to gently put those wavy fronds back in place, to trail his fingers over her cheeks for a moment as he did it, a familiar act like a lover or a husband might do.

He dragged his gaze from her. 'I'm going to take you home now,' he said.

'No, honestly, Alexander. There's no need. It only takes an hour for me to get back,' Sabrina said, but he interrupted.

'I do have an ulterior motive,' he said. 'If we go now, it'll give you a chance to freshen up before I take you out to supper.' He paused, looking down at her. 'I think you deserve a hearty meal—and the other day when I dropped you home I spotted a very nice-looking Italian place nearby...'

'Oh yes, that's Marco's,' Sabrina said. 'It's good. Melly and I go there sometimes.' *After I've been paid*, she thought. 'And we might discuss the next steps in chapter forty,' she suggested. 'Only if you want to,' she added hastily.

'Um, yes, we might,' he agreed. 'Or, there again, we might not. We might well feel we've had quite enough of that for one day. Besides,' he said as they left the kitchen together. 'I have another, slightly different, proposition to put to you. If it fits in with your personal plans,' he added enigmatically.

CHAPTER SEVEN

SABRINA had to admit that being driven home in Alexander's swish car could hardly be compared with her usual trek, involving walking and being squashed in the tube after a long day. As usual, the traffic was heavy, and it had gone six o'clock by the time they pulled up at the house. Sabrina's car was outside in its allotted parking space, but for once there was a spare slot opposite for Alexander to leave the Aston Martin.

He glanced across. 'Do we need to book a table at the restaurant?' he asked, and Sabrina shook her head.

'I don't think so, as it's Thursday. Weekends are always the busiest.'

Before he could get out, Sabrina opened her door and was already making her way up the short front path before he joined her. As they went inside, she looked up at him quickly.

'Do you want the TV on while I have a shower?' she asked, thinking that after the day she'd just had the thought of soaping herself under some nice, warm water was just what she needed.

'You carry on—don't worry about me,' he said casually, following her into the sitting room. 'Anyway, there's no rush, is there?'

Sabrina paused by the door for a second. 'Would

you like something to drink?' she asked, then thought, what could she offer him? She certainly didn't have a well-stocked cellar to choose from. But then Alexander came to her rescue.

'No, I'm all right, thanks. But why don't I make us a cup of tea?' he suggested. 'While you're freshening up.'

'OK, let me introduce you to the kitchen,' she said.

Although Alexander had driven her home once or twice, he had never come into the house before. As he followed Sabrina along the hallway it was no surprise to him to see how well-kept everything was. He was beginning to know her by now; the recent transformation she had made to his study told its own story.

'This is due for a refit,' Sabrina said, glancing around the kitchen, slightly embarrassed. 'I've been looking at home-improvement brochures to get some ideas.'

'It looks fine to me,' Alexander said. 'And perfectly adequate for two people.' He went over to the glass-panelled back door and stared out at the garden. 'Who keeps this tidy?' he asked, observing the rectangular piece of neat lawn accompanied by small groups of flowering bushes.

'Oh, we do. But it doesn't take long, not with the size it is,' Sabrina replied, taking down the tea bags and opening the fridge for some milk.

Leaving Alexander to it, she left the room and went upstairs, knowing straight away what she was going to wear. It would be a dress for a change, she thought, a special dress.

The item she took from her wardrobe was the one she knew suited her perfectly—a simple cream number, its flimsy, floaty skirt just reaching the knee, with a some-what dramatic gold pattern slashed across it at random intervals. Sabrina smiled as she remembered how Melly had described her in it: that it looked as if she'd been struck by lightning.

Soon, luxuriating under the shower, she leant backwards, letting the hot water drench her from head to toe. She remembered suddenly what Alexander had said earlier—that he had a proposition to put to her. What had he meant by that? Sabrina wondered. He hadn't taken it any further, and she hadn't asked him to explain. But she hoped it would be something that her circumstances could cope with; Melly was due home soon. But, still; Sabrina shrugged. She must try and co-operate with Alexander's requirements, she thought, because she was not going to give up this job with him for a long time yet. There was more money going into her bank account than she'd ever known before. Plus, she was getting used to seeing Alexander every day.

Sabrina bit her lip for a moment. During their telephone conversations, Melly had not once asked how Sabrina was getting on, how the new post was turning out for her. The talk had all been about Melly and how her life was going. But then, her sister had always been a bit like that, Sabrina admitted as she stepped from the shower and reached for a towel.

Downstairs, as Alexander sat idly watching the news with his mug in his hands, he suddenly heard a tremendous crash from above followed by an agonized shriek from Sabrina. Without hesitating for a second, he put down his tea and raced up the stairs, wondering what on earth he was going to find.

Sabrina was standing at the top clutching a huge white bath-towel around her, obviously very upset about something.

'What's going on?' he demanded. 'Are you OK, Sabrina?'

He swallowed hard. Her hair was streaming wet around her shoulders, making her look like a winsome nymph who had just emerged from a deep lake. He knew very well that she was naked and vulnerable under that towel. For a fraction of a second Alexander struggled with a natural impulse to pick her up in his arms and make love to her there on the floor at the top of the stairs...

'What's happened, Sabrina?' he repeated.

Without a word, she turned. He followed her into the bathroom, where he saw that a large mirror, still steamed up, had fallen from its place on the wall and had crashed to the floor, a huge, ugly crack right across its surface. Glancing at her quickly, he could see that she was visibly upset about it.

He stooped to examine the damage at the back of the mirror. 'There's the problem,' he said. 'The cord holding it up on the wall has frayed, that's all.' He glanced up at her. 'I'm afraid you'll have to buy another mirror, Sabrina, this one's had it.'

She shivered, her teeth chattering for a second. 'That's going to be seven years' bad luck, isn't it?'

'Rubbish,' Alexander said emphatically. 'You don't believe that stuff, do you?'

'Not really,' Sabrina said doubtfully, thinking that she and Melly didn't need any more wicked fairies planning unpleasant surprises for them. She smiled apologetically. 'Sorry to give you a shock, Alexander, but it certainly gave me one. I thought the roof was coming down on my head!'

He raised one eyebrow slightly. 'It was one hell of a

noise,' he agreed. 'I wondered what on earth could have happened.'

Suddenly, the position she was in caused Sabrina to flush to the roots of her hair. It seemed weird enough that her boss was here at all in their simple little home, but much worse was the fact that he was standing in the bathroom next to her, knowing that she had absolutely nothing on under the towel.

He bent down again and picked up the cumbersome mirror in his arms. 'This one's probably for the tip,' he said casually, noting the considerable damage to the frame. 'But fortunately the glass hasn't shattered, so there are no splinters for us to pick up.' He glanced back at her as he left the room. 'I'll bring up your tea,' he said briefly. 'It's getting cold.'

In her bedroom, Sabrina towelled herself as quickly as she could. It had never struck her that she should check the cords holding up all their pictures and mirrors, and she still felt unnerved by what had happened. She was especially unnerved because during probably the one and only time her boss would ever visit the house he'd had to witness the whole sorry thing.

Well, what was done was done, she thought. Now, slipping into her underwear, she switched the dryer to fast, brushing her hair out at the same time. It would just have to stay damp, she thought. She'd leave it loose to dry by itself, because she couldn't keep Alexander waiting any longer. Then she smoothed a trace of foundation onto her face and neck, adding a slick of eye shadow and a touch of blusher to her cheeks, before thrusting on her gold heels and going downstairs.

Alexander was lounging on the sofa, his long legs stretched out in front of him. Hearing her come in, he turned his head to gaze at her and for a second neither of them spoke. Then, 'You look beautiful,' he said briefly. He knew that he'd paid that same compliment to plenty of women in the distant past, but there'd never been a time when he'd meant it more.

Sabrina did look *divine*, he thought. That dress could have been made especially for her, and her hair—clearly still damp and floating loosely around her shoulders—made her look more seductive than she herself could possibly know. That was one of the things he liked about the woman—she seemed totally unaware of the effect she had on the people around her. Well, had on him, anyway, he admitted. And how had he allowed that to happen? he asked himself. He'd always held that mixing business and pleasure was a no-go area, well known to cause more trouble than it was worth.

They left the house and Alexander glanced down at Sabrina as they wandered along side by side, not touching.

'Won't you need a wrap of some sort?' he enquired casually, covertly admiring the creamy smoothness of her bare arms and neck, the glimpse of her delicate cleavage. 'I know we're having a phenomenally warm October, but it's bound to get cold later on.'

'No, I'll be OK—it only takes a couple of minutes to get to Marco's. And it's always pleasantly warm in there,' she replied, a little ripple of pleasure running through her at what he'd just said. It was so good to have someone—a drop-dead-gorgeous man like Alexander McDonald—be considerate of her in that way. It felt comforting, reassuring, and she suddenly felt more elated than she had for a long time. She realized just how much she'd missed going out on a date—if you could call tonight a date, she thought. Tonight was merely her boss's way of saying thank you for this afternoon's reading. But wasn't that what he was paying her for anyway? Perhaps this was by way of a bonus.

She knew that she was enjoying her present employment more than she could have dared to hope—and she had the distinct impression that Alexander wasn't finding her constant presence too intolerable. It might have been so different, she acknowledged, if he had turned out to be a creep like his brother. Well, that would have brought matters to a very rapid close. But thankfully, in that way, and probably many others, the two brothers could not be less alike.

As they entered the restaurant, the young, dark-eyed manager came forward.

'Hello, Signorina Sabrina!' he exclaimed effusively. 'We have missed you!' He was thinking that one of their favourite clients never came in with a man these days.

'Hi, Antonio,' Sabrina said. 'Um, this is Alexander—a friend,' she added, glancing at the two men in turn.

'*Signor,*' Antonio murmured, bowing his head deferentially.

'*Buona sera,*' Alexander said casually. Of course Alexander probably spoke the language fluently, Sabrina thought, and many others.

Antonio led the way to a candlelit table by the window. Alexander said, looking around, 'So, this is your local, is it, Sabrina?'

Sabrina smiled quickly. 'We don't come here all that regularly,' she replied. 'Probably once every couple of months or so. They're always so welcoming, though.'

It was on the tip of Alexander's tongue to say that Antonio could hardly be blamed for his flattery, with Sabrina looking as she did tonight. But, wisely, he kept quiet.

'I'm going to choose something rather good for us

this evening,' Alexander remarked, running his finger down the wine list. 'To celebrate the fact that we've kick-started chapter forty. I feel optimistic that with a bit of luck I can get it finished by the end of the month. Which is what the publisher expects,' he added.

Sabrina looked down for a second. *Did he say* we've *kick-started chapter forty?* she thought. Was that a slip of the tongue, was he being overly kind...or was she really that important to him? Either way, it gave her a thrill to hear him say it.

It didn't take them long to make their choice from the large menu, though Sabrina let Alexander lead the way. Well, he was paying, and she didn't want to select anything too pricey.

He decided they'd have Antipasto Misti to start, followed by Saltimbocca alla Romana—escalope of veal braised in Marsala wine, with ham and eggs.

'Does all that sound OK with you?' he asked, glancing across at her.

'Perfect,' she said, realizing that in all the time coming to Marco's she usually stuck to pizza or lasagne, which were the less expensive things on offer.

As they started on the second course, she glanced up at Alexander, suddenly feeling shy. He was incredibly handsome, she thought—not for the first time. He had such strong features, almost perfectly outlined, the firm chin already forming a fine stubble of dark, seductive hair.... But the mesmerizing feature had to be his eyes. Not just their intense, dramatic colour but the way he quite often used them to look at her. His thoughts behind that magnetic expression were unknowable, but it added to the delicious sense of mystery about Alexander McDonald which she'd been painfully aware of from the beginning.

Sabrina sighed inwardly as she picked up her fork again. No wonder he'd apparently spent half his life holding the female sex at bay, she thought. He could afford to pick and choose. For a second she felt almost sorry for Alexander McDonald. Too much choice became no choice at all, in the end. And what about that lovely girl in the snapshot who he'd been holding so closely, so intimately? What had happened to her? She obviously hadn't matched up to his expectations. Sabrina wondered whether there was a woman alive in the whole world who he could ever commit himself to. Somehow, she doubted it—anyway, hadn't he assured her after his mother's party that he intended to remain single for ever?

Sabrina put another morsel of veal into her mouth as her thoughts ran on. She didn't think that Alexander McDonald ever changed his mind about anything. Not once he'd declared it.

Briefly remembering that awful evening at his family home, Sabrina couldn't help comparing it with how she was feeling at the moment. Their supper afterwards at The Woodcutter had been good, and Alexander had been charming and conciliatory about what had happened. But this was different. She felt unexpectedly confident and happy to be here with her boss; she was enjoying every second of this occasion. And if he wasn't sharing her feelings then he was putting on a pretty good show, she thought. He seemed more relaxed than she'd seen him before. After all, this was his idea; there'd been no need for him to take her out and buy her dinner.

Interrupting her thoughts, Alexander said as he picked up his wine glass, 'I'm curious about something, Sabrina.'

She looked up. 'Oh? What's that?'

'You're the first woman I've ever been with—honestly, the first woman—who never wears any jewellery. Well, I've never seen you with any,' he added.

Sabrina smiled quickly. 'I do have some,' she said. 'And I used to wear some, now and then. But I made it my own unwritten rule never to have any on when I was on duty...in my other life,' she added. 'When in the company of patients, it seemed more appropriate to keep a low profile, to be sort of anonymous, to avoid distractions. The only noticeable person in any session should be the client—well, that's my opinion,' she added apologetically.

He nodded slowly. 'I take the point,' he said, thinking he should change the subject—quickly. He didn't want Sabrina—or himself—to think of her professional career; there was still so much *he* needed her for. But he knew the time was bound to come when she'd want to take off again.

And he wasn't going to tell her that, even as a small child, he was suspicious of anyone over-dressed. He'd never liked all the bangles and beads his mother was never seen without, nor the suffocating smell of the scent she insisted on spraying all over herself.

'What about perfume?' he ventured, instinctively thinking that Sabrina Gold was quite fragrant enough without it anyway. 'Does that come in the same category?'

'It does,' Sabrina replied, putting down her fork at last and sitting back.

It was dark by the time they left the restaurant, and as they walked back along the streets they could hear the sound of loud, gaudy music.

'Where's that coming from?' Alexander asked curiously.

'Oh, that must be the fairground—it's right over there in the municipal park,' Sabrina said. 'I'd forgotten that it always arrives in time for the half-term school break. Perhaps the warm weather has encouraged them to come earlier this year.'

'I haven't visited a fairground for ages,' Alexander said almost longingly, and Sabrina looked up at him in surprise.

'I can't imagine it would be your kind of thing,' she said.

'Well, you're wrong there,' he said. 'Let's go over and take a look…just for a few minutes?'

It didn't take long to reach it, and Sabrina could see at once that Alexander was like a boy again as they wandered amongst the crowds. The place was buzzing, with all the usual rides at full tilt; the nostalgic smell of the generators filled their nostrils.

'Fairgrounds have been around for generations,' Alexander said, drinking in the atmosphere. 'I hope they never go out of fashion. They're part of our history.'

At the far end was the ferris wheel. Suddenly Alexander took hold of Sabrina's hand, pulling her alongside him towards it.

'Come on, let's be daredevils.' He looked down at her. 'Are you game?'

Sabrina could hardly believe this. Was this her *boss* here with her, helping her into the seat, securing the safety straps around them both? But she was having fun, she thought to herself, feeling ridiculously child-like. And, noting Alexander's expression as he gazed out into the night, as the giant machine took them ever onwards and upwards, she knew that he was having fun too.

They reached the highest point, and as the wheel paused briefly to take on more customers, they could see the city's lights spread out beneath them like a magic carpet of stars. For Sabrina, it seemed an intoxicating moment, and she took a deep breath.

Then, just as they began moving again, a strong breeze caught them unawares, momentarily lifting Sabrina's dress right up, making her shiver. Immediately, she felt Alexander put his arm around her shoulder and pull her towards him. She instinctively responded, nestling into him, feeling her body ache for something more...

'I told you you'd need a wrap,' he shouted above the din of the music, still not letting her go.

'I didn't expect to be this far up in the stratosphere!' she shouted back, trying to pull her skirt down again. But she knew he'd seen her naked thighs, the edge of her underwear, and she bit her lip. This whole day was turning out to be surreal, she thought.

They eventually came back down to earth, and started to stroll back, neither saying much. Alexander looked down at her.

'Are you OK, Sabrina?' he asked.

'I'm fine,' she assured him at once. But she knew she wasn't fine at all. Despite having had a fantastic evening, she was full of guilt. She'd been enjoying herself with her boss far too much, and when he'd drawn her into him up there in the night she'd realized how much she loved the feel of him close to her, loved the masculine scent of him teasing her nostrils. And she knew this was wrong, wrong, wrong! How was she allowing such thoughts to intrude on her official status as his secretary? This could be a dangerous game, she thought, because she knew that her time with Alexander McDonald was going to be short—and inconsequential.

As they got back to the house, he said suddenly, 'Oh, I forgot to talk to you about something, Sabrina...'

This was obviously going to be the proposition, she thought, not looking up.

'Oh?' she said.

'Yes. I think I'm overdue for some respite time,' he said. 'At my place in France. It'll still be nice and warm there, and I'd like you to come with me. I'm already starting to think about the next project, the next big idea, and fresh surroundings might provide some fresh inspiration.'

They arrived back to where he'd parked the Aston Martin. 'We could leave at the end of the month,' he went on. 'It takes less than a day to get over there. We'd be away for perhaps two weeks... How does that grab you?'

Sabrina sighed inwardly. She'd never heard anything before about his home in France. She hesitated before replying.

'I'm not sure I could agree to that, Alexander,' she said. 'My sister will be back soon.' Sabrina crossed her fingers as she spoke. Making her sister an excuse could be a convenient ploy sometimes—because that was what it was. Sabrina's immediate reaction, not wanting to go to France, was less to do with Melly and much more to do with not wanting to be alone with Alexander away from work. Especially in *that* romantic part of the world. Her emotions tonight had been sufficient warning, surely?

'Well, give it some thought,' he said casually. 'I shall be going in any case. And I would hope that you *can* come,' he repeated.

They made their perfunctory goodnights, and
Sabrina let herself into the house, her mind in turmoil.
Everything had been going so well, she thought, until
Alexander had insisted on them riding on the wheel.
How could she have let Alexander's unexpected touch
cause such a titillating thrill of erotic excitement run
through her? Because he *had* excited her. For those few,
brief moments her body had ached for him. She shook
her head angrily. Was she really that susceptible?

As the Aston Martin sped through the now almost-
deserted streets, Alexander felt a sudden burgeoning
sense of optimism. He admitted that he did enjoy the
company of lovely women, something he'd deprived
himself of for a very long time. And his secretary had
shown him just how much he'd missed it.

He tapped his fingers on the steering wheel as he
waited for the lights to change. Although Sabrina hadn't
seemed particularly enthusiastic about his request that
she should go with him to France, he knew that his
powers of persuasion would probably win her over. She
was so genuinely eager to help him with everything he
asked of her, he could probably convince her that the trip
would be good for both of them. One of his reasons for
taking her was to give her a holiday, to give her a treat,
to give her the chance to relax and enjoy the peaceful
surroundings which he himself always found so thera-
peutic. And if anyone deserved a holiday, both from
emotional and business ties, then surely it was Sabrina
Gold.

And who better to spoil her and give her a really
wonderful time than Alexander McDonald?

CHAPTER EIGHT

SABRINA woke early the next day. As her eyes flickered open, she saw that the hands on her bedroom clock pointed to six a.m. and she snuggled back down for a minute, smiling to herself, remembering. She had dreamed the most wonderful, colourful dreams for most of the night, it seemed.

Then she sat up slowly, hugging her knees, a slight frown knitting her eyebrows. That off-duty time with Alexander had added a whole new dimension to what they had, she thought. She wasn't going to think of it as a relationship, because that word embodied something far too significant, too meaningful. But neither could she deny that a sea change had happened—at least to her. For the very first time since he'd been her employer, Alexander had shown her something of his very personal self.... Could she ever forget his touch, his caress?—that intimate caress? That was what it had been. As that fairground ride had swung them slowly backward and forward in the night-time breeze, he had held her to him possessively, keeping her warm and safe, not wanting to let her go. Another memory which would last her for a lifetime.

But what about this morning, when they came face to face? Would she be able to act casually, noncommittally? And would Alexander even remember the incident which had given Sabrina such erotic dreams?

One thing she had already made up her mind about: she was definitely not going with him to France. It was not only about leaving Melly by herself; it was because Sabrina could not afford her plans to be altered in any way, and she knew that being alone with her boss in one of the most romantic countries in the world could spell danger. How easily she had allowed her mind to wander last night. How easily she had succumbed to the briefest expression of physical contact with a man! Her frailty of determination had surprised her, and she shook her head briefly. She must see that she continued to remain single-minded, looked out for herself and Melly, and did not let any interruptions rock their boat.

Getting out of bed, she went across to the window and drew aside the curtains. There was another working day ahead of her; she bit her lip thoughtfully. She would tell Alexander straight away that she would not be going with him. How was he going to take that? And would he still pay her if she wasn't by his side? That was a worrying thought... But, then, she'd be here, wouldn't she? To answer the phone, check the Internet, maybe send any additional stuff over to the publisher if necessary, be a general dogsbody and keep the place ticking over... And Alexander could always send her any instructions he might have for her by email. Distance was no deterrent to progress these days.

By the time she got to number thirteen, Sabrina felt rational, cool, calm and collected—even though she was dreading having to tell Alexander her decision.

She waited a few moments for someone to answer the door; Maria had clearly already left, and presumably Alexander was out too—or maybe still asleep! Then she opened her purse for the key she'd been given, and let herself into the house.

She was beginning to feel almost as much at home here as in her own place, she thought as she went up the stairs, though she'd only ever seen the kitchen, bathroom and study. Pausing briefly, she glanced along the landing. There were three or four doors to other rooms on this floor, and presumably the same number on the one above. What a place for Alexander to rattle around in all by himself.

Did he ever feel lonely? she asked herself, before dismissing the idea. Alexander McDonald was a complete entity. He'd never need anyone to keep him company. The only reason she'd been asked to go with him to Lydia's party a couple of weeks ago had been made very clear at the time. And now his wish that she should go with him to France was for the same thing: he would find her useful to him. Any need was purely self-centred and work-oriented.

Shrugging briefly, Sabrina went into the study and as usual went straight over to open the windows. It didn't take her long to realize that Alexander must have been working late into the night—the unmistakable litter on his desk said it all. Glancing at her own, she saw a pad with his familiar scrawl on it; obviously the next part of chapter forty, she thought. Great! Because she was longing to know how the convoluted plot was going to unfold...

By now it was obvious that she was alone in the house. Alexander must have left very early—probably an extra gym-session. He hadn't bothered to open the mail, so for the next twenty minutes Sabrina checked what was in the post, then booted up their computers and made a note of the emails she knew Alexander would want to follow up. He was so selective in who he agreed to correspond with, she thought, it was surprising he had a friend left in the world. But he obviously did have, because there seemed to be so many who never gave up trying to contact him.

Suddenly, starting to feel over-warm, Sabrina went back downstairs to get herself a drink. For some reason, she hadn't wanted any breakfast earlier, having made do with a mug of tea, but it wasn't coffee she needed now—it was water. Cold, cold water. She went over to the tap to fill a glass, realizing that she was suddenly desperately thirsty. She drained it almost immediately, then reached over for a refill….

Now Sabrina knew that something strange was happening to her. Instinctively, she clutched the edge of the sink to steady herself, aware of her heart beating at a furious rate. She felt odd; her head was swimming, and the room seemed to be shifting under her feet…perhaps she was still at the fairground! But this wasn't funny, and she wasn't amused as panic began to set in. Things were not normal and she was no longer in control. She tried to take deep breaths, hoping she wasn't going to be sick in Alexander's immaculate kitchen.

With her legs now decidedly shaky, Sabrina went across to sit down carefully on one of the high stools…. Cross that; within just a few seconds her life seemed to be out of her own hands. Gently, she placed her forehead down on the granite surface of the unit, grateful for the momentary respite it gave her.

Then she heard the door open and from a very, very long way away she heard Alexander's voice.

'Sabrina! What… What is it?'

Raising her head carefully, she looked up to see him

striding over towards her. He was so unbelievably tall today, she thought, like…like a giant…

Then, just before he could reach her, Sabrina lost it completely and she began to slip from the stool, falling gracefully towards the floor. But before she actually hit the ground Alexander's strong arms were around her. She felt him lift her up towards him, felt the reassuring strength of his body enfold her, heard him call out her name urgently again and again, until, in a wonderful dream-world of unreality, Sabrina slowly drifted into unconsciousness.

Presently, when she finally came to her senses, Sabrina found herself flat on her back, gazing up at an unfamiliar ceiling. It took at least ten seconds before she realized what had happened to her and where she was.

She was on Alexander's king-size bed—well, she presumed it must be his—and he was leaning over her anxiously. As her eyes focussed on his, he gave a slightly awkward grin of relief.

'Ah, good. You've decided to return to the land of the living,' he remarked.

'What on earth…? What on earth happened?' Sabrina began, struggling to sit up, but he restrained her gently.

'Lie still. It's OK, Sabrina.' He paused, resting his hand on her forehead for a moment. 'I think you're beginning to cool down a bit.' He stared at her solemnly. 'Does this sort of thing happen to you very often?'

'What *did* happen?' Sabrina demanded. 'I was only…I remember getting myself a drink of water—and then I don't remember anything else.'

'Well, you collapsed fairly dramatically, that's what happened,' Alexander said. 'I came back just in time to catch you.' He shook his head briefly. 'You gave me the fright of my life.'

'Why? Were you afraid I was going to die before we'd finished the book?' Sabrina said, attempting a shaky smile. He didn't smile back.

'Why did you come in this morning, if you didn't feel well?' he said.

'But I *was* feeling well!' Sabrina protested. 'There was nothing wrong with me at all. And I can't remember if I've ever fainted before.' She swallowed, aware that her head was beginning to thump painfully. 'The only thing was, I didn't want any breakfast this morning, that's all. And then upstairs in the study I started to feel very thirsty…and the rest you know.'

But what she'd really like to know was how she'd managed to get up the stairs. Alexander read her thoughts.

'I'd thought you were coming round, once or twice, in the kitchen,' he said. 'Then I'd lose you again. So I thought I'd better get you up here to lie down for a bit.'

'How did you…?'

'I carried you, of course. You certainly weren't going anywhere under your own steam,' he replied flatly.

Sabrina let her thoughts dwell on the scene for a moment. She knew she didn't carry any excess weight, but still it couldn't have been an easy task for Alexander to lift her bodily and take her up that long flight of stairs. Or perhaps it was no problem at all for someone with his strong frame and wide shoulders, his muscular biceps…

'I'm going to take you home straight away,' he said. 'And you're not to come back in to work until you feel absolutely OK again.'

'But I'm sure I'm going to feel OK *now*,' Sabrina protested. She hated being ill; she wasn't used to it. And, anyway, there was only room for one patient in any household, and it had never been her.

He looked down at her thoughtfully for a moment. 'I hope we… I hope I haven't been expecting too much of you lately, Sabrina—not working you too hard,' he said. 'I can go on for hours without a break and sometimes forget that others might need to take things at a slower pace. Sorry, but you really should tell me if you're feeling tired.' He hesitated. 'I've never thought of myself as a slave driver—the only head I've ever beaten with a stick is my own—but maybe I am and haven't realized it.'

Sabrina smiled wanly. 'This is not your fault, Alexander,' she said. 'And you're not a slave driver. If I'd thought you were, I would probably have given you a sign of some sort.'

In a minute or two, Sabrina attempted to sit up again, then began to have the horrible suspicion that there was more to her situation than she'd thought. The glands in her neck were beginning to feel stiff and painful, and there was a strange, unfamiliar taste in her mouth.

'Oh dear,' she said faintly. 'I don't feel so good after all, Alexander.'

'No, and you don't look it,' he replied bluntly. He paused, gazing down at her, unfamiliar feelings of tenderness rippling through his body. He came to a sudden decision.

'I'm not going to take you home after all,' he said. 'You're going to stay here—at least for the weekend.'

As Sabrina started to protest, he went on firmly, 'Everyone's talking about this horrible virus that's going around like wildfire. And although I'm no medical genius it looks to me as if you might have it.' He put his fingers gently either side of Sabrina's neck 'Does that feel tender?' he asked.

Sabrina sighed. 'It does,' she admitted reluctantly. 'But honestly, Alexander, it's better if I go home.' She paused. 'I'm quite used to looking after myself, and you don't need me around.'

Oh, but I think I do, Alexander thought.

'Why go home to an empty house?' he demanded. 'Your sister won't be there, so you won't have her to worry about. Why turn down the chance for someone to look after you, for a change? Someone to make you hot drinks, maybe even bring you scrambled eggs in bed?' he added.

But he knew he wasn't thinking only of her. He was thinking of himself. He wanted to look after Sabrina, wanted to take care of her. Why had he never felt like this about a woman ever before? What had stopped him having those feelings?

In spite of not really wanting to fall in with his plan, Sabrina did suddenly feel drawn to the idea. He was probably right about her having picked something up. She looked at him, her eyes huge now in a face which looked pale and wan.

'But if I *have* caught this virus, wouldn't it be better for me to make myself scarce? Aren't you afraid of catching it?' she asked.

He grinned properly now, sensing that he was going to get his own way.

'Not a chance of that happening,' he said cheerfully. 'For some reason, I always manage to remain impervious to bugs of all kinds.'

But, rather worryingly, not impervious to the winsome charms of my present secretary, he thought.

Sabrina bit her lip. She obviously had nothing with her, no night clothes or toothbrush, and she hated being unprepared. Once again, Alexander read her thoughts.

'Sorry I haven't anything in the way of female attire to offer you,' he said. 'But you're welcome to borrow my T-shirts—which will reach your knees, I should think, so they shouldn't be too uncomfortable And there's a new pack of toothbrushes in my bathroom cabinet. Anyway,' he added, 'there's enough of everything for you to make do.'

By now, the idea of not having to go back home was becoming more attractive by the second. Sabrina knew without any doubt that whatever she had was not going to go away easily. She sighed, smiling up at him briefly.

'Well, if you're sure I shan't be, you know, interrupting your creative flow, Alexander, or be in the way…'

'Let's forget my creative flow for five minutes,' he replied firmly. 'Let's think about you, just you, for a change.'

The next twenty-four hours passed in a blur of semi-misery for Sabrina as she alternated between spells of uncomfortable sleep and fits of coughing that made her chest hurt. She felt very hot and very cold by turns, her subconscious mind an outrageous mix of noises and disruptive sounds. And all the time she was barely aware of Alexander silently coming and going into the room to place fresh water by her side, and to gaze down at her almost ghost-like appearance.

He had decided not to move her from his bed, and had used one of the spare rooms for himself. But he'd been so concerned about Sabrina that he'd hardly slept at all, tiptoeing in and out to check up on her.

At three o'clock on Sunday morning, he went in to find her sitting up, mumbling incoherently, her face flushed and her hair in damp tangles around her shoulders. Suddenly Alexander was angry with himself, really angry, that he hadn't called for his doctor to visit—though he could well imagine what Sabrina's reaction would have been to that suggestion. But what if she had something much more serious than they thought? What if this was the dreaded meningitis, or something else equally as dangerous? He would never, ever forgive himself if the worst possible scenario should take place under his roof—and to someone like Sabrina…all because he'd neglected to get professional advice.

Without saying a word, he picked up the glass of water by the bed and gently encouraged her to take a few sips. Then he laid her back down gently and went into the adjoining bathroom to rinse out a wet cloth to place on her forehead. Catching a glimpse of himself in the mirror, he thought *he* didn't look too good, either. His face appeared unusually tired and careworn. But then, he reminded himself, this was the first time he'd ever had to look after someone who was sick; he had never experienced these surprisingly deep feelings of closeness, of compassion, this longing to wave a magic wand and make someone better.

At least he was thankful that he'd managed to persuade Sabrina to stay here. It was unthinkable that she should be in this state alone at home.

Going back in with the cold, damp flannel, he placed it gently on her forehead, holding it there for a few moments. He realized that she seemed to be calmer now, her breathing less rapid, and he began to relax. Perhaps he was panicking unnecessarily; from everything he'd heard about the present infection, that was apparently decimating the population, Sabrina's symptoms were classic. And, if it was true to type, by the morning she should be over the worst.

That was how it turned out, because he went back in to find Sabrina breathing peacefully—having actually managed to sleep himself for a couple of hours—the hurtful coughing no longer punishing her slight body.

Sensing she wasn't alone, she opened her eyes and smiled up at him. Alexander was so relieved to see that she was definitely so much better, he could have rushed across and clasped her to him. It was the best possible feeling in the world, he thought, to know that someone you cared about was no longer in danger.

He sat carefully on the edge of the bed and took hold of her hand. 'Hello, Sabrina,' he murmured.

'Oh, Alexander. Where have I been?' she said. 'What day is it?'

'It's Sunday—at eight a.m. And I think you've been on an unexpected journey to No-Man's Land. But you're better now, or you will be soon.' He squeezed her hand more tightly and she sat up then, leaning her head on his shoulder for a second. The sight of Sabrina in his huge T-shirt—which had slipped off one side, exposing a smooth, tender curve of her breast—made Alexander's heart almost burst with tenderness. What power did this woman possess to give him such feelings? he asked himself. Was she a witch?

Later, after he had brought her tea and a thin slice of toast and marmalade, Sabrina felt sufficiently recovered to have a leisurely shower and wash her hair, which had become an unruly mass of tangles as she'd tossed and turned. By now she was just beginning to appreciate the position she'd landed herself in—albeit through no fault of her own. She had spent the weekend in her employer's bed, had apparently been watched over by him for many hours, and had sat up to obediently eat the first solid food she'd had for a couple of days while he'd just sat there, watching until she'd finished every crumb.

How on earth had all that come about? she asked herself. How had he persuaded her to stay here overnight—over two nights? It felt both strange and amazing at the same time. Alexander McDonald had taken care of her in a very personal way, while she'd been completely unable to do that for herself—something she never could have imagined in a thousand years! She shook her head briefly.

Life was so full of surprises, she thought, some ghastly, some exciting and pleasurable. Despite the fact that she'd been feeling so utterly wretched for two days, this latest episode in her life could easily be placed in the latter category! For her boss to stand over her in his dressing gown—as she'd been aware of from time to time—looking unusually unkempt and unlike himself was something she'd never expected to see. But all she knew was that it had made her feel grateful that someone else had taken control.

It was mid-morning by the time she'd dried her hair and got dressed, and although she still felt as if she was walking slightly above the ground Sabrina knew that she was well on the way to recovery. She also knew that she must go home soon and recharge her batteries in her own surroundings. She could get used to being here, she thought, glancing around at Alexander's luxurious bedroom. Unlike his study, everything was immaculate, from the expensive drapes at the window and the cream, fitted carpet on the floor, to the tasteful prints on the wall. And his bathroom was to die for, she admitted, thinking of her own—and shuddering at the memory of him standing there the other day beside her. Chalk and cheese was about it, she thought.

Then she squared her shoulders. Such thoughts were not allowed. It was useless to wish for something you knew could never be yours. She and Melly had enough of everything they needed. And they had each other.

She went downstairs; the smell of coffee coming from the kitchen was starting to wake up her taste buds. Alexander turned and smiled at her.

'Ah, that looks more like you, Sabrina,' he said, looking down at her approvingly. How could he have dismissed her appearance as irrelevant on that first morning in September? he asked himself. Sabrina Gold could never be thought irrelevant—in any way at all.

She went over to stand next to him as he made the coffee. 'Do you mind taking me home in a minute, Alexander?' she asked, wishing she felt strong enough to get back under her own steam.

'Why go back straight away?' he asked casually, not looking at her. 'I was thinking that after I've impressed you with my scrambled-egg dish we might have a run out in the country for an hour or so. It would do you good to have some fresh air—perhaps a stroll for ten minutes or so?' Now he did look at her. 'Unless there are urgent things for you to attend to, of course,' he added.

Sabrina knew that there wasn't anyone or anything urgent waiting for her at home, and in any case she still felt very fragile. What Alexander had suggested was suddenly very appealing.

'Well, that does sound rather attractive...' she began.

'Good. Then that's settled. The newspapers are in my

sitting room, next to the bedroom. Take your coffee up, and I'll start constructing the eggs.' He grinned down at her, thankful that Sabrina was obviously so much better—and pleased that she was ready to fall in with his plans for their day.

Sabrina did as she was told, finding that Alexander's sitting room was much as she would have expected. Again, beautifully, expensively furnished—but not without the tell-tale signs of someone who found that being tidy was an irksome task. But it was cosy, lived-in and lovely, Sabrina thought as she settled herself back down in the enveloping cushions of one of the large, deep-green sofas.

For the next few minutes she tried to read the newspaper, but found that she couldn't concentrate long enough to take anything in. She picked up her mug of coffee and sipped thoughtfully for a moment.

When was she going to pluck up the courage to tell Alexander that she was not going to France with him—after he'd just been so kind, so thoughtful? She could repeat what she'd already said—that Melly couldn't be left on her own for long. She could hardly tell him the truth. She could hardly say, *sorry, Alexander, you're becoming far too important to me. I am beginning to like you too much, to need you too much. And this is not the template for my life. You're cutting across my plans. And I must somehow put a stop to it before it's too late, because I believe that it won't take much for me to be seduced by you. To be seduced by my employer. And that's not good for business, is it? Not good for you, with your career to think of, and not good for me, who has vowed never to be emotionally involved with a man ever again.*

She would tell him later, when he took her home,

Sabrina decided—get it over with before she changed her mind.

Soon, she heard his voice from below. 'Breakfast is served, my lady!'

Smiling, she got up and went downstairs. As she reached the bottom, the front-door bell rang, and without hesitating she went to see who it was.

The smile on her lips died in an instant—Bruno was standing there. And, as their eyes met, his sly expression said it all.

'Well, well, well…' he drawled. 'I didn't think you were expected to work on *Sundays*, Sabrina.' He moved forward to come in. 'I told you he could be a demanding brute, didn't I?'

Almost at once, Alexander was behind them, and he didn't bother to couch his words as he stared at his brother with distaste.

'Didn't I make myself clear the other day, Bruno?' he said flatly. 'Didn't you get the message that I do not welcome unexpected visitors—whoever they are?'

Bruno smiled slowly, looking from Sabrina to his brother and back again.

'I can quite see why not,' Bruno said suggestively. 'And I'm sure it *is* a surprise, Alex, old boy,' he said. 'I've obviously come at a *very* inconvenient time.'

'Yes, you have. We're just about to eat our breakfast,' Alexander said, unsmiling. 'Even so, I would ask you to join us—but, sadly, I've used up all the eggs.'

'Oh, don't worry about me, Alex,' Bruno replied, totally unperturbed. He paused. 'Have you two been working all hours, then? You…you must have had quite a night.'

'Bruno, you wouldn't believe the night we've had,' Alex said solemnly. 'Which is why Sabrina and I need some nourishment to upgrade our energy levels. So I'm sorry to rush you away, but please have the grace to inform me the next time you're likely to call, won't you?'

And, with the briefest of goodbyes, Bruno was gone.

'Well, you know what *he* was thinking!' Sabrina said, following Alexander into the kitchen.

He looked down at her, with the heart-stopping twinkle in his eyes that sent delightful shivers right down her spine to her toes.

'What—that you spent the night in my bed?' He paused. 'Well, you did, didn't you?'

'Yes—but you know what I mean, Alexander. He's sure to jump to all the wrong conclusions.'

Alexander raised one eyebrow. 'Who cares?' he said. 'Now, come and eat your breakfast.'

CHAPTER NINE

THANKFULLY, the virus which had invaded Sabrina's body disappeared within two or three days, so Alexander's novel could progress unhindered.

He had been more than usually preoccupied with bringing his latest masterpiece to a successful end, and as they continued to work almost silently together in the study Sabrina made a point of keeping her head down and not intruding on his thoughts. She had learned by now when to keep quiet, when to make herself invisible, when sometimes not even to distract him by making them coffee or tea. And once or twice, when she'd arrived in the mornings, she'd been aware that he'd almost certainly been up most of the night, scribbling, crossing out—and no doubt cursing. But there was always the latest manuscript waiting for her to sort and print out, and he was keeping the promise he'd made—that it would all be completed by the end of October.

Now, as Sabrina saw the plot unfolding before her eyes as she typed, she had to admit that the conclusion was completely unexpected, with a totally amazing, unbelievable twist that brought a smile of satisfaction to her lips. This, then, was why Alexander McDonald's books never failed to impress—or to sell in shed loads.

She'd hardly seen him at all today, but now as she

handed over the final printout for his inspection she couldn't resist telling him how she felt.

'Alexander,' she said quietly. 'This is an amazing piece of work—and I loved the end. Just loved it! I'd had no idea how it was going to work out. How…how did you do it?'

He shrugged. 'Thousands of hours of practice,' he said. 'But thanks for the compliment, Sabrina.'

He looked down at her as he spoke, remembering just how ill she'd been ten days ago and how little fuss she'd made about it. He'd wanted her to have time off to recover properly, but she'd had none of that—and he didn't persuade her to change her mind. Because he needed her—wanted her—by his side. He could never have envisaged how indispensable this woman would become to him. How he looked forward to every day, just to see her, be close to her.

He had decided not to mention France again until after the novel was complete, but he was pretty certain she'd be coming with him despite her reservations about her sister. And it would do them both good to get away from here for a spell, breathe different air, he thought. Surely she'd see that?

He stood up and pushed back his chair. 'This is great, Sabrina,' he said, indicating the pile of papers in his hand. 'I'm going to take it over to the editor right away, and when I come back—I shouldn't be long—we might even open a bottle of champagne.'

Sabrina smiled up at him, pleased that he was so happy, so obviously content with all the hard work he'd put in over the last months. And, when he was happy, it made her happy too.

He turned to go. 'Oh, by the way, make some enquiries about flights to Carcassonne…say towards the end of next week? That would suit me, if it suits you.'

Sabrina paused before answering. 'I don't think I agreed to come with you, did I, Alexander?' she said carefully. 'Though it's very kind of you to include me in your arrangements.'

'It's got nothing to do with me being kind,' he said flatly. 'It's all to do with us both having a brief period of renewal. You've been putting in nearly as many hours as I have and you're due for a break. Especially after that bug you picked up.'

Sabrina stood up, pushing a stray frond of hair from her forehead. 'No. The thing is, Alexander, my sister texted me last night to say the group are due back on Sunday—a bit earlier than was expected. So I do need to be around for her for a while.'

'That's OK,' Alexander said, not to be put off. 'We can leave when we like—Wednesday or Thursday next week—and that'll give you three or four days to settle your sister back home, won't it? And it's still lovely in the Languedoc area in early November.'

Sabrina looked at him squarely. 'I really cannot say with any certainty that I can come,' she said. 'I've already told you, I need to be here for my sister's return.'

'Well, she certainly seems to have done all right without you in Spain,' Alexander said bluntly.

'So it would appear,' Sabrina retorted. 'But I would still like to see her.'

'And that's understandable,' Alexander said, trying to sound reasonable, even though he couldn't see why someone of twenty-six couldn't be left in her own home for a couple of weeks without her big sister holding her hand. 'And you *will* be there—for several days—to make sure everything's OK.' He paused. 'I'm sure your sister would like to think of *you* having some time away, too.'

Sabrina looked at him for a moment, biting her lip. This exchange between them wasn't going too well at the moment, she thought—especially as she couldn't give Alexander the other rather important reason why she didn't want to go to France.

'Well, all I can say, Alexander, is that my instinct is that you will be going to France without me. But,' she said quickly, seeing the handsome face darken, 'I will think it over. And, anyway, I'll still be here when you get back. In the meantime, I'll see that everything ticks over—check the post and the web. I might even do a bit more cleaning up in here!' she said, trying to keep things light for a second. Alexander McDonald was used to having things all his own way, to not having his plans upset, and she could see from the expression on his face that he was annoyed with her.

'Well, in my opinion, I think you should give your sister the opportunity to stand on her own feet for once,' he said. 'It seems to me you've been a kind of crutch to her for too long—always dependable, always there to sort out her life. From the little you've told me about her Spanish assignment, she's been doing very well, thanks. Sometimes, Sabrina, love is shown in the letting go—so I've heard. Are you sure this isn't more about you than her?'

That hurt! And Sabrina had been listening to what he was saying with growing anger and dismay. How dared Alexander McDonald interpret her life like this? What did *he* know? Well, he'd blown it now, she thought. She was damned well not going with him—anywhere! Who did he think he was? Let him stick to his fictional characters and their problems, and leave her and Melly out of it.

She managed to keep her voice calm. 'I'll bear your opinion in mind,' she said coolly. 'And I'll come to my decision about France in due course. And you'll be the first to know,' she added.

And with that she left the room, shutting the door with an unnecessary bang, and went downstairs to make herself a cup of tea.

Later, alone in the study, Sabrina felt somewhat at a loose end now that the novel was finished. She'd almost felt the tenseness lifting from Alexander as he'd come to the end of it—but he'd already stated that ideas for the next one were beginning to boil in his head; she knew it wouldn't be long before it was a case of *déjà vu*.

After busying herself with the filing, which had been woefully neglected of late, she took some invoices from his personal file and started to write out the necessary cheques for him to sign later. She was just finishing the last one when the phone rang. It was Alexander.

'Sabrina,' he said. 'I'm afraid I'm going to be held up here for a bit because we're waiting for the publisher to put in an appearance.' He paused. 'You go on home. And, look—have tomorrow off. That'll give you a nice long weekend to prepare for your sister's homecoming.'

Was he being sarky? Sabrina thought.

'Oh, OK, then,' she said coolly. 'Thanks.'

'No—thank *you*, Sabrina,' he said. 'The final draft has been approved, so it's all smiles here. I think we can congratulate ourselves.' He paused. 'Sorry about the champagne, but I'll keep it on ice. Oh good—they've just arrived, so I'll have to ring off. So, see you Monday,

Sabrina—and I hope you find your sister in good spirits on her return.'

Sabrina put the phone down, biting her lip. His hurtful remarks earlier had cut into her deeply—but was he right? Had she assumed for far too long that Melly couldn't survive without Sabrina being on hand all the time? And most awful thought of all—one which had only just taken root in her mind—had Melly in fact been a surrogate child, the child Sabrina had always longed for?

The possibility that Alexander might have a point made a considerable impact on Sabrina; wasn't she supposed to be the psychologist? Wouldn't she have worked out the true position for herself by now? But maybe perceptions were dimmed when you were too close to a situation, she agonized; objectivity could often take a back seat when it concerned you and yours.

With her thoughts running in all directions, Sabrina rested her head on her hand. Why not forget what Alexander McDonald said, just for a moment? she told herself. Melly would be back home in three days—and how was she really going to be? It was true that she'd given no indication that anything might be wrong, or that she was unwell, but Melly was a clever actress, and could be confusing sometimes. She would have realized that, even if she had been unhappy, there'd have been nothing Sabrina could do about it. Maybe her apparent enthusiasm had all been a sham because she didn't want to worry her sister. The two girls had never been apart for this long before; how would Melly have survived this totally new dimension to her life?

With her head beginning to ache now, Sabrina stood up suddenly. It was all very well for Alexander McDonald to offer his illustrious opinion, but his own family values were hardly creditable. They were feeble, in fact. He didn't know what he was talking about.

In his editor's office, as they uncorked a good bottle of wine, Alexander's mind was only half on the discussions going on around him. He wished he hadn't said all that to Sabrina, about her and her sister. The moment he'd uttered the words he could see the hurt spread across her features. And she was an intelligent woman; she didn't need him butting in. Especially as he knew very well that the real reason he'd done it was because he'd been angry with her. Angry that, for the first time, he'd almost put his heart on the line, and Sabrina had said No. He'd been silly, childish and unfair, and he wished with all his heart that he could rewind the tape. The thought that he'd made her unhappy—even for a second—was unbearable.

One thing was certain, he thought grimly. She'd never agree to come abroad with him now. And much, much worse—what if she decided she didn't want to work for him any more? What if she gave in her notice?

With yet another stab of genuine surprise at the intensity of his feelings towards her, Alexander realized that being without Sabrina Gold in his life was unthinkable.

Early on Saturday morning, the telephone by her bed rang and Sabrina sat up to answer it, rubbing her eyes. It was Melly.

'Sabrina? *Hello!* Oh, Sabrina, I've had the most marvellous time, and there's so much I have to tell you!'

Sabrina couldn't help smiling. Her sister was on cloud nine, obviously. 'Won't it wait until tomorrow, then?' she asked mildly.

Without a pause, Melly said, 'No, not really. Well, let's just say that *I* can't let it wait until tomorrow!'

'Go on, then,' Sabrina said. 'Fire away.'

And Melly did fire away, her words coming out in a rush. For the next twenty minutes, she gave Sabrina a blow-by-blow account of everything that had happened on the trip, hardly stopping for breath. She was deliriously excited; a transformation had taken place.

'I've never had such a brilliant time in all my life, Sabrina. And the thing is, well, I—me and Sam— remember you met Sam?—we're not coming back tomorrow with the others. Not for a couple more weeks.'

Sabrina sat up properly then, utterly bewildered at this sudden change of plan.

'Perhaps you'd better explain,' she said.

Melly took an audible, deep breath before going on.

'It's Sam and me—that is, well, Sam has just been wonderful the whole time, Sabrina. I think I'm in love with him.' She paused. 'In fact, I know I am. I've never felt like this about a man before; I've never met anyone like him before. And I know you're going to say it's a passing holiday-type thing that has no future, but I know differently. And so does Sam. We like the same things, we laugh about the same things…we're just on the same wavelength! All the time! And, well, I hope you won't think I'm being stupid, but…'

Sabrina got out of bed, clutching the phone more tightly in her hand. Spain had certainly had a very dramatic effect on her sister.

'I'm not thinking anything,' Sabrina said. 'You're twenty-six years old, Melly. It's time you began to interpret your own emotions and not rely on me to do it for you all the time.' She paused. 'What has Sam said to you, exactly?'

'He said that he wants us to get to know each other better, spend more time together. And not only that— he can almost guarantee me permanent work with his team. And, the thing is, he needs to stay on here after the others have gone back home—there's more work for him—and he wants me there as well. By his side,' she added. She paused. 'He really is lovely, Sabrina, and I know we love each other. Really I do. And you're going to love him too, when you get to know him.'

For a few moments, Sabrina felt almost bowled over by all this. Melly had had one or two minor relationships in her life before, but had never expressed her feelings in such extravagant terms.

'You don't think I'm being silly, do you, Sabrina?' Melly repeated earnestly. 'And—do you believe in love at first sight? Sam does, so he told me. And I think I do, because he's on my mind all the time. I just want to be with him.'

Thinking over what her sister had just said made Sabrina feel envious…just for a second. 'No, I don't think you're being silly,' she said slowly. 'And I…do believe in love at first sight. But I don't think it happens every day—and when it does it should always be treated with a certain degree of caution.'

'That's exactly what Sam said! We won't rush things; we'll value each day as it comes. And I've been managing everything fine so far, making the clothes I brought with me last—well, there are laundry facilities here, of course. And I've also bought a couple of T-shirts. And because I've been paid my wages I don't need to ask you for any more money—which I'm sure you're glad about!' she added.

Suddenly, Sabrina felt completely anonymous, as if she wasn't there at all, as if she was hearing everything from a long way off. She recognized that, through Melly, she was experiencing again the euphoric joy of being in love. She could only hope that her sister's expectations wouldn't be dashed to the ground—for whatever reason. Life could be so unfair, so unpredictable. What if Sam wasn't all that Melly thought he was? He wasn't exactly young—probably nearly ten years older than her sister—and would have known plenty of women. He was an attractive man. She sighed inwardly. The last thing Sabrina needed was to have to pick up the pieces of Melly's life again if this all came to nothing.

Neither of them spoke for a few moments after that; Sabrina wondered when her sister might be interested enough to ask about what had been going on here at home, or how Sabrina was getting on with *her* job.

Presently, Melly said, 'Oh, how's your life—your job—going, Sabrina?'

'Ticking along,' Sabrina replied carefully. 'In any case, it's only pro tempore, as you know, until I get back to my proper job. I'm not really sure how long this one's going to last—it could end at any time—but the pay is more than enough to cover the mortgage and all our other bills at the moment, and that's a very comfortable feeling.'

'Well, it looks as if I'll be able to add to our coffers myself as soon as I get home, Sabrina,' Melly said. 'Because Sam's promised me plenty of work, so I'll be earning good money for a change.'

Suddenly, rather like she were witnessing a warm sun emerge from behind a cloud, Sabrina said, 'By the way, Melly, I'm going to be away myself, just for a short while. It's a work thing,' she added. 'I think we're leaving for France on Thursday—probably back mid-November. So I may not be here when you eventually get back. Is that OK?'

'Of course. And how lovely for you, Sabrina! Have a great time, won't you? But don't let them work you too hard, will you?' Melly giggled suddenly. 'Something else I forgot to say—do you know, Sam only lives a mile away from us? He told me he's been jogging past our house every morning for the last year! Isn't life amazing?'

'Oh yes—it certainly is amazing,' Sabrina said faintly.

CHAPTER TEN

ALEXANDER paid the driver of the cab which had brought them to the airport, then he and Sabrina trundled their cases towards the entrance. He glanced down at her, noting that she'd pulled her long, fine-wool cardigan closer around her.

'Yes,' he said. 'There's definitely a colder feel to the air now. But don't worry; where we're going it's still lovely and warm. I checked it out last night.'

As he guided Sabrina in front of him through the revolving doors, he was still amazed and elated that she'd agreed to come with him, almost at the last minute. But, after all, she *had* promised to be his PA, hadn't she? His right-hand woman in every way? Though, taking her abroad had never been on his agenda... He rarely invited anyone to the Barn, relishing the peace and solitude of the place, his escape route from everything and everyone.

But Sabrina was different. She was the only woman he'd ever known who he'd not quickly grown tired of, who'd never, ever, got on his nerves. And as that thought struck him, he realized that surely he must be partly to blame—that he was the one out of step, not womankind in general. It was just that so many of those he'd met all seemed to fit into the same mould as Lydia—taking everything for granted, never satisfied for long, restless. There *had* to be women who were different, who shared his values, his perspective on life. Well, of course: wasn't she here, right next to him?

They made their way through the crowded aisles and were shown into the lounge for business-class passengers. In spite of all her earlier reservations, Sabrina couldn't help feeling upbeat. It *would* be good to have a change of scene, even though she'd had second thoughts after telling Alexander on Monday that she'd go with him, mostly because, judging from her latest phone call, Melly had been unstoppable, incorrigible, in her new-found euphoria. Sabrina was waiting for the bubble to burst, for the girl to come back down to earth.

For his part, Alexander had been wise enough not to show undue surprise that Sabrina was coming with him—and not to look smug, as if as usual he was going to have his own way.

'Oh, fine,' he'd said, noncommittally. 'Let's go Friday, shall we? And why don't you have Wednesday and Thursday off, so you'll have time to get ready.'

Her sister was, apparently, not coming home just yet—which fitted their—his—plans perfectly.

Now, as they took their places in the aircraft, Sabrina had to admit that Alexander always managed to surprise her. He exuded such power and confidence, he almost gave the impression that he could take over from the captain. Sabrina found herself basking in the comforting warmth of being with someone who was taking control of everything, who was planning out every move ahead. All she had to do was to sit there and enjoy it. She could get used to this state of affairs! she thought.

As the plane droned its way towards their destination, Alexander glanced across at Sabrina, feeling proud to have her sitting by his side. She was wearing black, slimline trousers and a white scoop-neck top which exposed the tantalizing smoothness of her skin. With her hair coiled up on top of her head, she managed to look both smart and casual at the same time. It was the first time he'd seen her in high heels; her black patent-leather shoes completed her stunning appearance. How did she always manage to look just right? he wondered. Was there ever a time when she was caught unawares, or at a loss? Then Alexander smiled to himself, remembering her reaction when her bathroom mirror had crashed to the floor.

'Have you done much travelling? Have you been to France?' he asked her casually.

She turned from gazing out of the window to look up at him. 'Yes, to Paris,' she replied. 'Melly and I had a five-day break there a few years ago, and we went to Brittany once or twice when we were young. But we know home shores better than foreign ones.'

'Well, it'll be great to show you the part of France that suits me best,' he said. 'Still basically unspoiled, and the perfect place to unwind.' He smiled. 'We do have a few neighbours, but no shops, I'm afraid—so, if you'd hoped for some retail therapy while we're away, you're going to be disappointed.'

'I'm not a great shopper,' Sabrina said. 'So that won't be a problem.'

She didn't bother to add that earlier in the week she had gone into town for a couple of new things to bring away with her. Having agreed rather reluctantly to come on this trip, she'd made sure she wouldn't run out of clothes before the end of it.

The flight only took a couple of hours or so, just long enough for them to enjoy the wine and the light lunch which was served to them. Only ever having flown economy class before, Sabrina couldn't help comparing the two. There seemed so much less hassle, she thought, and the extra space made all the difference. Especially to someone like Alexander, who had no difficulty in stretching out his long legs and relaxing.

'I've packed my laptop in my case—' she began, and he interrupted her.

'Why? This is supposed to be a holiday.'

'But—but I thought it was partly about your next novel. That's what you said, Alexander,' Sabrina replied. 'You said you were hoping to find fresh inspiration…'

'Oh, did I? Well, maybe I will, maybe I won't—with an emphasis on the latter,' he said breezily. 'I intend to be thoroughly lazy and drink a great deal of wonderful wine—and I hope you're going to join me,' he added, smiling slowly into her upturned face. 'And we'll take it in turns to rush out for fresh baguettes every morning, because at exactly nine-fifteen Claudette arrives in her little white van with fresh supplies for the locals—and she doesn't hang around. Three sharp beeps on her horn, and you've got about two minutes to join the queue before she makes a fast getaway.'

Picturing the scene, Sabrina couldn't help smiling. 'Are there really no shops—even food shops—then?' she asked.

'Nope. The nearest supermarket is five miles down the road, where we can restock everything now and then,' he said. 'But we'll be OK for the first few days because two of my neighbours, Marcel and Nicole, will have made sure we won't go hungry. They're a great couple—you'll like them. They look after my place for me when I'm away, and stock up the fridge to greet me when I come back.'

'It sounds an ideal arrangement,' Sabrina said. 'You're lucky that they're around to do it for you.'

'It is,' he agreed. 'And I am. And I bet they'll insist we have dinner with them tonight—they know I'm bringing someone with me this time.'

Sabrina looked away as he spoke. Who did he usually bring with him? she wondered. Was there a special female that no one knew about? She kept remembering that beach photograph; when, and where, had that been taken? Then she shrugged inwardly. From Alexander's youthful appearance on the snap, it was clearly taken rather a long time ago.

But Sabrina admitted that she was curious about her employer's personal life. Although he'd stated that he intended to remain single—for ever, he'd said—there were bound to have been many other women. Someone with his masculine appeal could have the pick of the bunch. Whatever he'd said to her, it certainly didn't mean that he never enjoyed the full company of a female when he felt like it. And where better to do that than in an isolated place in rural France? There wouldn't be any photographers popping out from behind bushes to catch him unawares and provide gossip for the media. Was this his real purpose in asking her along? If so, she'd make sure she wasn't another notch on his bedpost!

As she dwelt on all this, Sabrina wondered whether she'd made the silliest mistake in her life by coming with him. His apparent reason for inviting her had been that it would not only be a chance for a rest, but that they might do some work in relative peace. But now, apparently, he'd changed his mind about doing any writing.

The flight was smooth and uneventful, and as they came into land Sabrina stared down in fascination at the medieval city of Carcassonne. Alexander touched her arm. 'We'll spend a day there before we go back home,' he said. 'It's something not to be missed.'

At the airport, Alexander had made arrangements to hire a car, and as they fastened their seat belts he said, 'It takes about forty-five minutes to get to the Barn, so sit back and enjoy the scenery.'

The roads were blissfully uncluttered, and from the effortless way Alexander negotiated the twists and turns it was obvious that he must have made this trip scores of times.

'Where is everybody?' Sabrina asked, staring out of the window, and Alexander chuckled.

'That's just the point—there isn't anybody,' he said. 'That's why I come here.' He glanced across at her briefly. 'Though that's not strictly true, of course. We'll be going through some little villages in a minute, and nearer the Barn you'll see the huge hypermarket on the horizon.'

In almost exactly the forty-five minutes Alexander had said it would take them, Sabrina could see a cluster of buildings ahead, and soon they arrived at a small hamlet of about half a dozen dwellings. 'This is it,' Alexander said briefly.

As he drove slowly up the poorly maintained road, Sabrina couldn't help feeling rather surprised. It was hardly the most inspiring scene in the world, she thought, noting that the heavy door of every building they passed looked as if it hadn't seen a coat of paint for years, and almost all the walls seemed to be flaking and unkempt. *Hardly Alexander McDonald territory*, she thought.

He pulled in and switched off the engine. 'Welcome,' he said.

Inside, what a different world, a magnificent conversion from what had once been a farming necessity!

It was spacious and airy, with polished hardwood in evidence everywhere. As Alexander showed Sabrina around each room it was obvious to Sabrina that, for him, this was home from home.

There was a huge dining area with a refectory table large enough for at least ten people, and at the end was a fully fitted kitchen. On the same floor were two *en suite* bedrooms and a wet room, and tucked in one corner was a sizeable, partly obscured area for a television and a sophisticated sound-system.

Alexander led Sabrina up the beautifully crafted oak staircase to two more *en suite* bedrooms. At the end of the landing a pair of full-length windows opened out on to a balcony, from which the patio and swimming pool beneath could be seen, and ahead in the near distance was an uninterrupted view of rows and rows of vine trees and olive groves.

Almost lost for words, Sabrina looked up at him. 'Alexander,' she said slowly. 'What an absolutely lovely place.' She thought, *never judge a book by its cover!* How could she ever have guessed what lay beyond that rather scruffy front door?

'I had a feeling you might like it,' he murmured.

Then, they went down to the lower floor and made their way through the games room, complete with table tennis and snooker tables, and out on to the patio.

'I usually swim most mornings,' Alexander said casually. 'And, if it's hot, several other times of the day as well.' He smiled down at her. 'I told you it would still be warm here. Marcel told me on the phone that it's been a good year for weather.'

If she'd had any worries about coming here, those worries had suddenly disappeared! This was a magical place; who couldn't be happy here just for a couple of weeks? *I'm going to enjoy every minute of this totally unexpected holiday*, she thought. *And I have no fears where Alexander McDonald is concerned, either... I know exactly how to take care of him, if I have to!*

'What a lovely surprise that Alex has brought...a *friend* with him this time,' Simone said, pouring another glass of wine for Sabrina and pushing it along the table towards her.

Alexander had been right when he'd said there would be an invitation for dinner from the French couple, and Sabrina had to admit that Simone and Marcel LeFevre were everything he'd described.

The pair were in their fifties, Sabrina guessed, Marcel a dark, swarthy, good-natured man, his wife a rather round-figured woman with light-coloured, frizzy hair and shrewd blue eyes.

Their home was a pretty, ancient farmhouse with swimming pool—obviously not as grand as Alexander's. But their table groaned beneath delicious, unusual cheeses, a massive langoustine soufflé and salad, and home-made pastries straight from the oven to eat with crème fraîche and sweet almonds. And there was wine, and more wine, and rich, sensuously aromatic coffee. Would she need another thing to eat ever again? Sabrina asked herself.

It was getting late, and the two men had gone out onto the patio to chat, Marcel puffing happily on a cheroot. Simone leaned forward conspiratorially, her perfect English prettily laced with her own accent.

'Alex told Marcel on the telephone that he was bringing someone with him this time, but we never thought it would be a beautiful woman,' she said. She paused, unashamedly looking Sabrina up and down. 'I feel so glad, because as soon as I saw him today he looked different. Not so...sad, as he usually does.'

'Sad?' Sabrina said curiously.

'Oh, *mais oui*! Yes, sad, *chérie*,' Simone said emphatically. 'We have talked about it many times, Marcel and I, and always thought it was to do with the writing—his head always in another world, he has no time to think much about the one he's living in.'

Sabrina thought about that for a moment.

'His home—the Barn—is very big, just for him, isn't it?' she said. 'Doesn't he ever bring anyone here with him?'

'Never. Always alone,' Simone said. 'He has lent it to one or two friends in the past—and his brother came here once with a woman—but Alex seems to like being here alone. Which doesn't seem *natural* for a man, not natural for someone like Alex.' She smiled quickly. 'Have you known him a long time?' she ventured curiously.

Sabrina smiled back, not minding the question because it was obvious that the woman had a real liking for Alexander, cared about him.

'About six weeks,' she replied. 'I'm his secretary.'

'Ah, *ça va*? His secretary...' Simone said, nodding her head slowly.

'And the only reason I've been invited,' Sabrina went on, 'is because we've had a very busy time of late. Alexander has only just completed the latest novel and things have been a bit tense recently. So he thought we both needed a break—and, as it happened, my own circumstances allowed me to accept his suggestion.'

A slight frown crossed the knowing features. 'You—you have someone...?'

Sabrina smiled. 'No—at the moment, I'm quite free,'

she replied, wilfully misunderstanding Simone's enquiry. 'For a little while, I'm fun and fancy free!'

Simone's expression cleared. 'I am so happy to hear that,' she said. She stood up to fetch more coffee from the stove, and turned to look at Sabrina. 'I hope you will have a really good time here,' she said. 'You and Alex… together. He deserves someone to teach him one or two things.'

'I'm not sure what you mean by that,' Sabrina said, smiling.

'To teach him how to be a living person—a man,' Simone said firmly. 'And to open his heart.'

Only a French person could have said something like that, Sabrina thought, shrugging inwardly. She wondered how much of Alexander's past Simone and Marcel knew—about his parents, of the rather strange relationship Lydia had with her sons.

'Oh, I don't think we need worry about Alexander,' Sabrina said lightly. 'I'm sure there have been many women in his life.'

'Ah *oui*, of course!' Simone agreed firmly. '*Affaires*…naturally! But, love?' She nibbled thoughtfully on another almond. 'I am talking about the sort of love that only happens in sound relationships: family ties—commitment.'

'I've the feeling that Alexander would rather have a fit than a family!' Sabrina said, smiling at the thought. 'I'm sure he could never tolerate children getting under his feet. In that respect, he's the typical loner, I'm afraid,' she added.

Simone sipped at her wine. 'You're wrong, Sabrina,' she said. She put her glass down and leant forward, her elbows on the table. 'Our first grandchild was born a couple of years ago, and she was about six months old when Alex saw her. My daughter brought her over for a visit, and he was here. And he was—how shall I say?—*enchanté*! He could not take his eyes off her! And he has showered her with gifts ever since. In fact, he is godfather to our precious baby.'

Sabrina could hardly believe this. Alexander and... *babies*?

'I hope he didn't drop her at the font,' she said only half-jokingly, and Simone threw her hands in the air.

'Drop her? He handled that child as if he'd had six of his own! It was difficult for anyone else to get a look in, because he wanted her all to himself!'

If Sabrina had just been told that Alexander McDonald had beaten Edmund Hillary to the top of Everest, she couldn't be more surprised at what Simone had just told her. But before any more discussion could go on, the two men came in from the patio.

'I'm suddenly beginning to feel rather tired,' Alexander said, smiling down at Simone. 'Thanks largely to that magnificent meal, Simone. Thank you so much; as usual, we shall be returning the compliment before we go back home.'

Simone stood up and put her hands on his shoulders. 'You know how much we love your visits, Alex,' she said fondly. 'You don't come nearly often enough. And it has been a great pleasure to have a lady to talk to this time.'

'Well, if you want to keep good staff you've got to treat them well,' Alexander said, smiling briefly at Sabrina. 'Sabrina and I have been keeping our heads down for too long lately.'

After making their goodnights, Alexander led Sabrina the short distance between the two properties. Sabrina admitted that she, too, was looking forward to some sleep. Earlier, she'd been more than relieved to be shown her own room on the first floor; Alexander apparently always slept on the one above. She'd been prepared for the possibility that he might have expected her to share.

As they let themselves into the Barn, Sabrina glanced up at him.

'Why do you go in for such massive properties, Alexander?' she asked casually. 'This is huge. And so is number thirteen, of course.'

He paused outside her bedroom, looking down at her thoughtfully for a second. 'Because I like space, that's all,' he said. He waited a moment before murmuring, 'Goodnight, Sabrina. Sleep well.'

Then he turned and went upstairs, and Sabrina heard his tread on the wooden stairway. Slowly, she went into her room and closed the door.

Snuggling down under the luxurious duvet, she tried to imagine which room Alexander was sleeping in. Was it directly above her own, or the one further along? She hadn't quite got a handle on the geography of the place yet.

It had been a rather wonderful day, she thought sleepily. There was not a single thing she could complain about, anyway. The journey had been pleasant, and Alexander had acted the perfect gentleman the whole time, making her feel comfortable, unthreatened, and for some reason sublimely happy. She smiled faintly in the darkness, remembering everything Simone had told her. Alexander McDonald cuddling a baby in his arms! What a preposterous thought!

The other slightly less preposterous thought was that, if he'd wanted to seduce her, it wouldn't have taken him too much effort, she admitted!

* * *

In his own room, Alexander glanced at himself in the mirror as he brushed his teeth vigorously. Despite Sabrina's initial reluctance to come with him, he knew that she was happy to be here…happy to be here with him. And he also knew that he felt happier than he had for a very long time. She was the first person he'd ever invited to have a break here with him; he'd never wanted to share that solitude he so valued. But, for once, he *wanted* to share—and, if he'd been presented with a vast selection of other human beings to consider, Sabrina would have been his first, his obvious choice.

CHAPTER ELEVEN

THE first thing that Sabrina was aware of the next morning was the sound of three short blasts from a horn outside in the road. Of course: the van bringing fresh bread for breakfast. Well, she'd never make it in time to buy any! She hoped Alexander didn't expect her to take first turn, anyway—even though she must remember that she was still his secretary, his Jill of all trades.

But the next moment, after listening to several excitable voices raised in spirited greetings outside, she heard the heavy door slam and Alexander's swift tread coming towards her room.

Not bothering to glance at herself in the mirror, Sabrina shrugged on her dressing gown, opened the door—and came face to face with Alexander, who was clutching two large French sticks and a paper bag of something or other.

'Your turn tomorrow,' he said, smiling down at her in one appraising glance. The flimsy dressing-gown she had on revealed the tantalizing shape beneath, and her hair—tousled untidily and loose around her face, which was still pale from sleep—caused his senses to spin in mad circles for a second. He swallowed.

'Did you sleep well?' he remarked casually.

'Like the proverbial top,' Sabrina replied. She hesitated. 'You've clearly been up some time?'

He was bare-footed, his muscular legs brown and glistening, and he was wearing white shorts and a navy T-shirt. His hair was wet and plastered to the sides of his face which was unshaven, a strong line of dark hair shadowing his chin.

'I've been in the pool for half an hour.' He paused. 'But I wasn't going to wake you; we had a long day yesterday.' He turned to go. 'I was just coming to tell you it's nine-thirty already, so let's have breakfast.' He turned to go. 'And don't bother to get dressed now,' he added over his shoulder. 'You can take your time later. All this'll be ready in five minutes.'

Doing as she was told, Sabrina went back into her bedroom to sponge her face and hands and brush her hair quickly, before going through to join Alexander in the kitchen. The glorious smell of percolating coffee drove her tastebuds crazy.

He had cut the baguettes into generous slices, and laid out butter, jam and honey. Sabrina realized that she was feeling really hungry by now. Especially when she saw the two still-warm pastries he'd bought as well.

'After that wonderful supper last night, I didn't think I'd ever want to eat again,' she said, sitting down at the table and watching as Alexander poured the steaming coffee into two huge, wide cups. He passed her some milk and sugar and sat down opposite.

'Ah well, that's what French air does for you,' he said. 'Plus being totally relaxed and with no pressures.'

He was right, Sabrina thought as she spread butter onto a slice of bread. She did feel relaxed, had never felt more relaxed in her whole life. She suddenly seemed to be inhabiting a whole new world where nothing really mattered, quietly amazed at how quickly she and her employer had somehow adapted their relationship. She had that strange feeling once again that they'd known each other for ages. She shrugged inwardly. Perhaps that had something to do with the nearly three days spent ill in his bed.

Later, choosing to wear her dark-green cut-offs and an ivory, loose-fitting top, Sabrina slipped on her flip-flops and went downstairs.

'I think I'll show you the area, drive you around a bit this morning,' Alexander remarked, glancing across at her briefly. She was wearing her hair in one long, thick plait down her back; however she did it, it always seemed to suit the contours of her fine features perfectly—and to leave those intriguing green eyes room to express themselves in a way which fascinated him as much now as it had on the first day he'd met her.

'Sounds great—whatever you say, Alexander,' she replied, going over to the window and gazing out. 'I am in no position to argue about anything,' she added, smiling, thinking just how much she was enjoying the present situation.

'I can't imagine a time when you wouldn't be prepared to put your point of view, Sabrina,' he said, coming up to stand alongside her. 'But in this instance I shall take complete control of our day—and you can complain later if you haven't enjoyed it.'

The rest of the morning was spent idling through the local countryside. Although it was pretty deserted, as Alexander had said it would be, they did pass along a few clusters of dwellings, and the occasional small garage.

'Do you, um, do you ever bring other friends here?' Sabrina asked casually, not looking at him.

'Certainly not,' he said as if she should have known that without asking. He clicked his teeth, irritated for a second as he recalled the hundred and one hints Lucinda had made in the past about wanting to visit the Barn with him. 'I've just remembered something. Lucinda—you will recollect having met her, Sabrina?' This was said with a sardonic twist to his mouth. 'Lucinda is about to celebrate a rather important birthday soon, I believe. I received my gilt-edged invitation to what will be a ghastly event just before we came away.'

'That should be fun,' Sabrina said noncommittally.

'Probably not,' he replied. 'But, as I shan't be going, it's irrelevant.'

'I know where I'm going to buy you lunch,' Alexander said. 'It's a pretty little place, and the village has a rather interesting *château* on the hill.' He turned to smile at her briefly. 'The French are big on *châteaux*,' he added. 'But the restaurant right by the canal is the one I've used before—food's good.'

As they meandered along lazily, Sabrina could easily see why Alexander loved this area so much. You couldn't get much further away from civilization, at least as they knew it. But it was interesting scenery, vastly populated by olive trees and vine groves, separated now and then by a narrow river. Suddenly they came upon a small village which, surprisingly, had quite a large shop in the middle of the street they drove along. It had paintings in the windows, and various items of craftware displayed outside. Noticing her leaning forward, Alexander immediately slowed down.

'Do you want to look?' he asked.

'I'd love to,' Sabrina said at once. 'I suppose somewhere like this is bound to attract artists,' she said, and he nodded.

'Oh, there are several forms of cottage industry around and about,' he said. 'And the French have a formidable eye for business, as I'm sure you know.'

He parked the car and they wandered along, browsing curiously as they went and passing one or two interesting-looking cobble-stoned alley ways before coming to the shop.

'It's a surprising place—and there's lots more to see inside,' Alexander remarked. After they'd looked at the paintings in the window, they went through to be greeted effusively by a young Frenchwoman.

'*Bonjour, monsieur, mademoiselle...*' She smiled, indicating that they should come inside.

'*Bonjour*, Colette,' Alexander said easily. He glanced down at Sabrina. 'I know you said you were no shopper, but this could well lead you astray, Sabrina,' he added, before wandering off by himself to look further inside.

Sabrina had to admit that he had a point. It was a fascinating place, much larger than it appeared, and opening into other, smaller areas. For the next half an hour she enjoyed herself picking things up and putting them down again, studying everything that was on sale and wondering whether to buy or not to buy...

As well as quite expensive water-colours, there was a rack of woven scarves and shawls, a display of hand-painted plates, vases and pots of every description. There was a section for local jars of honey, of garlic bulbs in oil, of cherries in syrup, and rows and rows of home-baked biscuits in polythene wrapping. And in a corner by the window there was a display of brightly

coloured, hand-made jewellery, all glistening in the pale
sunlight.

She'd been so engrossed in looking around that she'd
only been dimly aware that Alexander was further in
the shop, having a lengthy conversation with the owner.
But just then he emerged, smiling, and glanced at what
Sabrina had in her hands.

'Have you made your choice, then?' he enquired,
and Sabrina handed a scarf and bangle to the French
woman.

'Yes, thanks,' she said. She looked up at him. 'Have
you bought anything?'

He nodded briefly. 'Oh, just a small present I needed
to get, but it's rather bulky to take back with us so
Colette's arranging for it to be shipped home later,' he
said.

Well, that was obviously some little gift for Lucinda's
birthday, Sabrina thought. He might not intend to go
to her party, but the woman would certainly expect
a decent present from someone as rich as Alexander
McDonald.

Colette wrapped Sabrina's gifts carefully before
handing them to her, and Sabrina took some euros from
her purse. 'You have a lovely shop,' she said, and the
woman smiled, darting a quick glance at Alexander.

'*Merci, mademoiselle,*' she said. 'Please do come
again soon.'

They went back to the car, and just after one o'clock,
they arrived at the other, slightly larger village which
Alexander had told Sabrina about. He pulled up outside
a restaurant which had a few tables outside standing
under brightly coloured canopies which were moving
gently in the breeze.

Across the road and through the trees, Sabrina

could see a canal glinting in the sunshine with a well-maintained longboat idling on the water and one or two small craft floating nearby. She was struck again by the whole atmosphere of stillness and quiet. She thought, *I could get to love this place, too.* Time really did seem to stand still.

They strolled over to the restaurant and took their places at one of the tables outside. There were one or two other people already eating, and immediately a waiter came up with a menu. Soon, Alexander and Sabrina began to enjoy the fluffy omelettes they'd ordered, complemented by a bottle of good wine and some cheese.

Leaning back in his chair and watching Sabrina finish the last of her food, Alexander wondered, not for the first time, what lucky chance had sent his current secretary into his life. He hadn't found a single fault with the way she did her work, or with her attitude at all times. But best of all, he realized, he loved her company.

They left the restaurant a little later and began to walk up towards the *château* Alexander had talked about. This once-beautiful residence, resembling those constructed during the Renaissance, had been built by a noble family but was now largely in ruins. It was a somewhat austere, turreted building standing right on the cusp of the hill, and suddenly the sun went in and Sabrina felt a chilly breeze around her bare arms. She reached into her bag and took out the scarf she'd bought.

'I think I'm going to need this sooner than I thought,' she said, coiling it around her neck and shoulders, and Alexander nodded briefly.

'Well, it is November, and it can get cool quite quickly,' he said. 'I hope you came prepared for all weathers.'

'I most certainly did,' Sabrina replied, thinking of the thick sweater she'd brought with her.

There was only a small party of French schoolchildren there as well, and Alexander and Sabrina wandered mostly uninterrupted through thick, stone entrances and gaunt passageways, before deciding to go back to the Barn.

'I think I feel ready for my swim now,' Sabrina said as they drew up outside.

Alexander smiled across at her. 'And I'll join you,' he said. 'After I've made us a cup of tea.'

Later in her room, as she slipped into her black one-piece bathing suit, Sabrina admitted to feeling worried about everything—about Alexander, and about herself. Because, heaven help her, she knew that she desired him... She'd have had to be made of stone not to want him to touch her, to make love to her—and she had to keep reminding herself over and over again not to get carried away. She did not want, did not need, any emotional turmoil or entanglements with him, or with anyone, that could lead to more disaster in her life.

She went barefoot into the bathroom to fetch a towel to take downstairs, her mind still darting every which way. The good thing was, Alexander had behaved impeccably, almost impersonally, since they'd left the UK. They'd barely brushed against each other at all, she realized, hardly made any physical contact. So, if she'd thought he had an ulterior motive in asking her to come with him, she was obviously mistaken. But every instinct told her that for her part she'd better keep any romantic notions—and her emotions—well under control.

Unfortunately, over the following few days the weather deteriorated considerably. But Alexander and Sabrina were still able to enjoy their morning swim in the warm water of the pool, and go for long walks; Alexander was clearly intent on showing her this part of the country he loved so much. They also drove to the coast on the one afternoon when the sun reappeared. There was certainly no talk of any writing being done.

They'd been there for more than a week when Sabrina's mobile rang. That could only be Melly, she thought, who'd rung a few days ago to say that she and Sam were back in the UK.

But it wasn't Melly; it was Emma, one of Sabrina's past colleagues who'd been lucky enough to be retained, telling her that an opportunity was coming up which Sabrina should apply for.

'It's a new thing they're initiating,' Emma explained. 'And they've actually got the funding this time, surprise surprise. And it's just up your street, Sabrina. As soon as we were told about it, your name was on everyone's lips. But you'll have to apply formally. Shall I get the stuff for you and send it over to your house?'

It took Sabrina a few seconds to get her mind into gear. She hadn't given her own profession a thought lately. 'I'm on holiday in France at the moment, Emma,' she said. 'But we'll be home at the end of next week.'

'Who's *we*?' Emma asked.

'Um, I'm here with my employer, actually—it's a sort of working holiday. Look, I'd be really grateful if you would send me the application form,' she added quickly.

'Course I will. Final date for submission is thirty-first of December.' There was a pause. 'And I'm glad you're having a break, Sabrina,' she added. Emma had known Sabrina for several years, knew about the problems with her sister and about Stephen's dreadful accident.

Alexander and Sabrina had been reading and listening to music, and now he looked across at her as she snapped her phone shut.

'That was one of my old workmates telling me about a post coming up that I should apply for,' she said briefly, picking up her book again.

Alexander resumed reading his magazine. 'Oh? And…are you going to?' he enquired, as if it was the last thing in the world that interested him.

'Oh, I shan't know until I've learned what it's all about,' Sabrina replied. She turned a page casually. 'Shall we have that steak we bought yesterday for our supper?'

'Sure,' he said, though wondering whether he'd have any appetite to eat it. His spirits had dramatically plummeted at the thought that Sabrina might even be *thinking* of leaving him—leaving him to pursue a different path, which would mean he wouldn't be seeing her every day, that she wouldn't be there any more.

Much later after supper, as they were sitting under the heater by the pool, Sabrina turned to glance at Alexander. 'I don't want to spoil your well-earned rest, Alexander,' she said. 'But have you given any thought to the next blockbuster? I told you I'd come prepared to do some work.'

'I haven't thought about it at all,' he said. *No—all I've been doing is enjoying myself here with you, Sabrina, with someone who feels like a part of myself.*

'Well, I just thought it my duty to mention it,' she said lightly.

It was past midnight before they left the poolside and climbed the stairs to the first floor where Sabrina slept. Before going up to his own room, Alexander paused briefly.

'Sabrina, thank you for another perfect day,' he said softly, and she turned to look back at him.

'Alexander,' she said. 'Any thanks are due to *you*. And...you're giving me such wonderful memories to take back with me.' She smiled tentatively. 'They're going to last me a lifetime.'

Silence between them hung in the air like a question waiting to be answered. Then, totally unable to stop himself, Alexander moved slowly over to Sabrina. Bending his head, he parted her lips with his mouth and kissed her fully, expertly, aware of a surging tide of passion tightening his groin. And, with her eyes closed against the intensity of the moment, Sabrina felt her senses exploding into a state of helpless longing....

Then, gently, he released her and without another word went upstairs. Sabrina heard his bedroom door close softly.

With her heart beating violently in her chest, she went in and sat on the edge of her bed, watching her knees trembling uncontrollably.

That was a *terrible* thing to have happened! she told herself, knowing that she should never have let it take place. To allow her boss to kiss her, really kiss her, in an unbelievably heart-stopping way, was pure madness! Their relationship—association; whatever the word was—was going somewhere neither of them wanted. Well, she was sure *he* didn't want it, and she couldn't *afford* to want it! They could never have a business arrangement now, after that, surely?

After a few moments, Sabrina felt her heartrate lessen and she stopped trembling, a feeling of quiet resignation sweeping through her. She knew that those erotic few moments just now had ruined all her good intentions, put paid to her common sense. She knew just how much she'd wanted it to happen deep down, had longed for it. To be held in Alexander's arms and feel his body press against hers had been bliss, pure bliss, proving once and for all that she must face up to things, to the inevitable. She was tired of running away; she'd been doing it for too long.

After a few moments, she got up and left the room— not even stopping to close her door—and slowly climbed the stairs towards Alexander's room. Without bothering to knock, she went inside, closing the door behind her.

He was standing by the window, and when he heard her come in he turned and looked down at her, a slow smile touching his seductive lips.

'Alexander,' Sabrina said, her voice cool and steady. 'Would you mind helping me undo this little hook at the back of my neck?'

CHAPTER TWELVE

AFTER a few seconds of complete silence, Alexander came over towards Sabrina, his arms outstretched. As he reached her she collapsed against him, automatically resting her head on his neck, a long sigh escaping her lips. They stood there, motionless, not uttering a word, letting this first breakthrough in their unspoken need for each other take them over.

Then with casual ease he picked Sabrina up, carried her over to the bed and sat down alongside her. Sabrina dropped her head forward so that he could undo the hook of her top, and as she felt the warmth of his hands on her skin a raging tide of feeling surged through her, making all her senses crawl erotically, making her whole body limp with surrender.

With infinite patience, Alexander slipped off her top and released the clasp of her bra, cupping his hands under her aching breasts and dropping a tender, lingering kiss on the back of her neck, making Sabrina want to cry out with desire.

Slowly he began to undress her, then laid her down on the bed before removing his own clothes until he, too, was completely naked.

For several breathless moments, he gazed down at her, drinking in the beauty of her tender curves, the smooth creaminess of her skin, and his eyes glittered like granite, glittered bright with heady anticipation. With wide and misty eyes, Sabrina looked back at him, the open, tender curve of her lips inviting him to take her...

Then Alexander lay down beside her and, taking his time, began to slowly explore her body with gentle, thrilling caresses, before his mouth, hot with passion, travelled from her lips to her neck, to her breasts and the flat plane of her stomach.... Their hearts raced in tandem as they trembled on the edge of fulfilment.

In a state of dizzy euphoria, when time seemed to stand still, Sabrina felt herself drifting on a cloud of pure ecstasy as Alexander's expert, unhurried love-making made every nerve in her body deliciously painful. Then he raised himself up and over her, and she felt the hardness of his muscles tight against her until, with irresistible grace and confidence, he slipped inside her. She clung to him with desperate exhilaration, her whole world seeming to explode into a vast display of starstudded emotion.

For a long, long time they lay clasped in each other's arms, neither wanting this magical experience to come to an end, but eventually he eased himself away and lay down beside her again. Then he brought her head onto his chest, holding her to him protectively, and gave a long sigh of emotional revelation.

As a pale moon shafted its gentle beam on to the lovers, they gave themselves over to a glorious sleep, a sleep which was filled with colour, wonder and total release.

When Sabrina awoke, dawn had barely broken; realizing that she was alone, she sat up, rubbing her eyes. Then she took the huge duvet which had covered them all night and wrapped it around her, before hobbling over to peep out of the window. It had been the sound of water being thrashed about which had roused her, and she smiled faintly as she saw Alexander, half-submerged, thrusting forcefully towards the far end of the swimming pool directly beneath the window. Then he turned and swam back, his powerful stroke covering the distance in a matter of seconds, before swimming back again and again… Perhaps all this activity was to make up for his lack of gym sessions, she thought.

He swam to the side, treading water for a second. Sensing that he was being watched, he glanced up and smiled, waving briefly before resuming his powerful overarm stroke.

He knew he had needed to do this, to energize, to be on his own to think about what had happened last night. Because where should he go, what should he do now? he asked himself. Although Sabrina had left him in no doubt that she had welcomed his ardour—and had returned it with a passionate lack of inhibition—he had no idea what to do next. What, if anything, did she expect would happen now? When they got back to the UK, would the situation be what it had been before— business as usual? But for him that would be unthink-able. He could not bear to be near her and not be able to hold her in his arms; he didn't have *that* much will power! But Sabrina had told him that no other man would ever claim her as his own, that that part of her life was over.

He cursed inwardly. Had he taken her by surprise, was it something which she might already be regretting?

And, worse, would she feel in the cold light of day that he'd taken advantage of her?

He lessened his pace for a few moments, his brow clearing slightly as he remembered. After all, it was she who had come to his room last night. Yes, it had been supposedly for him to help her with that hook on her top, but she'd never asked for his assistance before. And the hook was a simple enough one to undo; she could have done it easily by herself.

Well, he had taken it as an invitation, and he hadn't waited for a second one. There was less than a week before they returned home. Had he spoiled the remainder of their holiday together? He was feeling as insecure as a teenager after a first date. Still deep in thought, he swung himself out of the pool.

From her vantage point, Sabrina saw him walking towards the door to the games room. He was without swimming trunks, and her helpless gaze was riveted to his bronze, muscular body, the powerful strength of his physical being ravishing her senses once again.

Turning quickly, Sabrina remembered that she, too, was naked and should get back to her own room. But almost before she could reach the door he had opened it, and they stood looking at each other. Then, as if making a sudden decision, he went over to her and kissed her gently, once, on the mouth.

'You should have joined me—the water was perfect this morning,' he said lightly, as if what had happened last night had never taken place.

Sabrina swallowed, then said shakily, 'Do you mind if I borrow this for a minute?' pulling the duvet more closely around her.

'Feel free,' he said, going towards the bathroom to

shower. 'And I'll take your turn to fetch the bread this morning,' he added.

Picking up the clothes she'd had on last night, Sabrina turned and made her way down to her own room, feeling dizzy with mixed emotions. She hadn't known how he would treat her this morning, but one thing was crystal clear: his incredible love-making was par for the course. Today he'd barely looked at her—not properly, not meaningfully—and that swift kiss just now was merely a little acknowledgment that they were on slightly more personal terms than they'd been before; that well, hey, casual love-making was what people did, what grown-up, sophisticated people like him and the women he knew did.

As she showered and got dressed, Sabrina suddenly felt a huge wave of depression flow over her. Last night had been a wonderful miracle cure for all ills, but today she was completely downbeat, a state she rarely allowed herself to sink into. And it didn't take long to work it out.

Alexander's need for her was purely superficial and meant nothing to him. And why should she be surprised? He liked women well enough—he'd admitted that a long time ago—but only up to a certain limit. And that limit had been reached in the privacy of his room last night. So, having known all that, why had Sabrina allowed her own need to lead her astray? She had walked right into it, had walked uninvited into his room, and her not-so-innocent request that he undo the hook on her top had had the result she'd hoped for. So what was the problem?

She knew the problem. She was not needed by anyone in the emotional sense. Not by the man she was hopelessly in love with and now, apparently, not by her sister either.

For the first time in both their lives, Melly seemed to be standing perfectly well on her own two feet without Sabrina there to support, encourage and patch up.

Stepping out of the shower, Sabrina reached for a towel and began to dry herself. Pausing reflectively for a second as she caught a glance of herself in the mirror, she remembered Alexander's rather hurtful words the other day about her relationship with her sister. Perhaps he'd been right after all—perhaps it was a specific need, that she'd made herself more or less indispensable to Melly when it was being proved that she was not indispensable at all. But, what she really was, was guilty. Guilty of being over-protective, of stepping forward when she should have stepped back sometimes.

Well, Sabrina thought, she was beginning to see the light. About everything, about everyone. She was wising up, mostly about herself. And she might as well accept it: emotionally, she was not essential to anyone. They could all do without her, thank you very much.

Sabrina straightened her shoulders. She'd faced up to reality many times before in her life and she was good at sorting herself out. She'd do it again. There was still plenty of world out there waiting for her.

And, as far as her employer's future professional needs were required, he'd be able to find someone else, some other PA, easily enough when the time came. Just as he was going to have to do when—fingers crossed—she secured that post on offer.

On the last night in France, Alexander invited Marcel and Simone over for supper.

Sabrina had decided on her menu—chilled prawn

bisque to start, followed by blanquette of veal with fresh vegetables, and a Victoria sponge-cake with cherry sauce and cream for dessert. And, as Alexander was no cook, he'd been only too happy to let her get on with it and confine himself to selecting the wine.

For Sabrina, spending some time shopping and cooking was a welcome break from having had rather too much free time. She'd never been this long without having things to do.

Now, as she spooned the sponge mixture into the tins carefully, she felt relieved that they were going home tomorrow. It wasn't that she hadn't enjoyed herself, but ever since their fateful love-making things had been different between her and Alexander. He had seemed to be deliberately careful not to touch her much, and hadn't made a single move that could be interpreted as amorous. And she certainly hadn't invited herself into his room again. It was hard to actually describe the position between them, she thought. Their attitude towards each other was warm enough, and once Alexander had put his arm around her waist briefly. But she did feel that a sea change had taken place, that the waters had been temporarily ruffled and were now flat and calm again—with nothing to show there'd been any disturbance at all.

Yes, it was time to go home, she thought as she slid the pans of cake mixture into the oven to cook. But what was she going to find when she got there? Melly's new man might be sleeping under their roof for all she knew—how long might that be for? If he was, would Sabrina feel like an intruder in her own home?

Much later, with Sabrina's menu exclaimed over, and after every last morsel had been eaten, Simone and

Marcel made moves to go home. Simone put her arms around Sabrina and hugged her tightly.

'It has been good, *très bon*, to meet you, *chérie*,' the Frenchwoman said. 'And so good that the Barn has been occupied—even for a short time.' She paused, darting a quick glance at Alexander. 'You will bring Sabrina back again soon, won't you, Alex?' she said. 'Your lovely home needs to be lived in, and we love having you as neighbours. So…why not come for Christmas? We do Christmas very well here. Our little hamlet looks like fairyland with all the lights, and we all go carol singing, and eat and drink far too much! Do say you will come, *mon ami*?'

Alexander grinned down at Simone. 'I'll give it some thought, Simone,' he said. 'But I don't know whether Sabrina would want to come with me; she has family at home who need her, would expect her to be there at that time of the year.'

Sabrina looked away, not bothering to respond. She had no doubt that as far as Melly was concerned this year it would be two's company, three's a crowd.

'Well, anyway, before Christmas comes Sabrina and I have some serious work to do,' Alexander said. 'Two weeks off are as long as I can afford.'

After the couple had gone, Alexander and Sabrina cleared up the supper things together, and as he wiped the last of the wine glasses he glanced down at her.

'You've made a definite hit with those two,' he said. 'Marcel couldn't keep his eyes off you, and Simone has taken a real fancy to you as well.' He paused. 'I shall be got at now, and nagged every time I ring them, to bring you back here.'

Sabrina smiled at his words but said nothing, and in a minute he went on.

'I've never spent Christmas here myself, but from what Simone said it sounds as if it might be OK. Maybe I'll give it some thought.' He paused. 'But I suppose you'll be needed at home to cook the turkey, Sabrina?'

'I have a feeling that there could be a distinct change in routine this year,' Sabrina said casually. 'But I don't want to think about Christmas…not yet. Christmas is a long way off.'

'Not all that long,' he countered. 'And before that I've got to get started on the next novel. And I always crack on pretty well with the first section, so you'll be kept busy too.' He deliberately avoided mentioning the phone call from Sabrina's ex-colleague about a possible appointment. Let sleeping dogs lie, he thought.

'So I'm needed at my desk on Monday, then?' Sabrina asked, thinking that that would give her less than forty-eight hours to collect her thoughts, do some washing and assess the situation at home.

Alexander put his hands firmly on her shoulders and looked straight into Sabrina's eyes.

'You are,' he said flatly. 'And for as far into the future as it is logical to expect.'

CHAPTER THIRTEEN

As they took their seats in the plane at Carcassonne, Sabrina didn't know whether she was glad or sorry to be leaving France.

She had to admit that Alexander had gone out of his way to see that she relaxed and enjoyed herself, showing her all around the area he loved so well. And she had enjoyed herself. He had been the perfect escort and companion—and, yes, the perfect lover, she thought. Their one romantic night together would stay in her memory for ever. But the thing which had made Sabrina feel dismal ever since that poignant time was that no words passed between them to reassure her, to tell her something. Physically, he had expressed his ardour—wasn't that enough? For her, it was not enough and never would be. He hadn't said, in the heat of their coupling, *I love you, Sabrina*—words she'd hoped he might say. But it had been a vain hope; she realized that. It was not Alexander McDonald's way, and never would be.

She sighed briefly. The uncomfortable conclusion had to be that on that magical evening he had needed her—they had needed each other—and that need had been fulfilled. Totally. And that was that. Now, it was back to reality, work and the status quo.

Yet, even if their love-making had been a superficial

event for him, Sabrina didn't regret a thing. How could she regret being made love to by someone like Alexander McDonald, who had proved himself passionate, thoughtful and tender? Glancing up at him now, as he was putting their in-flight bags in the locker, she wondered if he'd actually thought about it at all afterwards. There'd certainly been no indication that he had.

Sabrina decided to get a grip on herself, on reality. She would consign the whole experience to her precious box of memories and get on with her life. She'd had a wonderful holiday; she'd met the lovely LeFevre couple, and for the first time ever she was expecting to go home and not have to worry about her sister.

They were waiting at the carousel for their cases when Alexander's mobile rang. He raised his eyes at Sabrina as he answered it; he'd left it switched off for most of the holiday, but now it was possible that his publisher might appreciate a word.

It wasn't his publisher, it was Lydia.

'Alex! Oh, thank God! I've been trying to reach you for two days.'

'Sorry, I've been having a bit of a break, Lydia. What's the matter?' It was obvious that something was wrong.

'It's Angus. He had a heart attack on Thursday and he's still in Intensive Care and...'

'Where is he—where are you?' Alexander demanded. Looking at him as he spoke, Sabrina could see the shock on his face.

For a few moments she heard Lydia's near-hysterical voice at the other end.

'OK, Lydia, I'll be with you in—' he paused to glance at his watch '—about an hour. We'll come straight over.'

There was another pause. 'Tell Dad... Tell Dad I'm on my way.'

He snapped the phone shut just as their cases appeared in front of them, and grabbing his and Sabrina's in his strong grip, he looked down at her.

'My father's had a heart attack,' he said briefly, and for the first time since she'd known him Sabrina saw a look of real fear, real concern, on the handsome features. 'We need to get to the hospital—now,' he added briefly.

Sabrina had to trot alongside him to keep up as they made for the exit, and as they reached the taxi rank she said, 'I'll find my own way home, Alexander.'

'No, you won't. I want you to come with me...please,' he said bluntly. Sabrina thought, well, yes; maybe there was something she could do to help.

It took less than an hour to get to the hospital, then they quickly made their way up the flight of stairs to the private room which had been allocated to Angus. As they almost ran along the corridor, Sabrina felt her stomach lurch with dread. She hadn't visited a hospital for a long time....

Almost immediately they were shown into the darkened room, and Lydia got up from her chair, her face a mixture of torment and despair. 'Oh, Alexander, I'm so glad to see you...' The words came tumbling out. 'It's been such a terrible shock—Bruno came to the hospital with me when it happened, of course, but he's got a raging flu and they've instructed him to stay away.' Clearly overwrought, she put her hand on the edge of the bed to steady herself for a second. 'Naturally, I haven't left Angus since he was brought in here, but...'

Alexander led his mother gently back to sit down. 'Now, Lydia, start from the beginning,' he said quietly.

Feeling slightly as if she was intruding on a personal family affair, Sabrina stood listening as Alexander's mother told him what had happened.

For several moments he let Lydia tell him the details—how Angus had come back from one of his regular trips abroad, hadn't felt very well after supper and had collapsed.

'I thought I'd lost him then, Alexander,' Lydia whispered. 'I couldn't pick him up from the floor and he looked so…so awful. He's come round once or twice, but he doesn't know me, Alexander. He doesn't know me….'

Now the tears began to flow, and Sabrina frowned slightly as she watched the scene in front of her. From what Alexander had said, it was not a particularly loving marriage, yet his mother was clearly distraught at the thought she might lose her husband of so many years.

Alexander went silently over to the bed where his father lay, and for several long moments just looked down at the inert figure. Then he caught hold of Angus's hand in both of his and started rubbing it gently.

'Hello, Dad,' he whispered. 'It's Alex…. Can you hear me, Dad?'

Just then, a young nurse came in followed by the doctor, and for several minutes they had a subdued discussion with Alexander, while Lydia sat like a crumpled bundle of clothes in the corner, just staring into space. Gone was the extravagant make-up, the ostentatious clothes; she was dressed in a plain navy skirt and jacket, and she didn't seem to have registered that it was Sabrina who'd come with Alexander. But then, she thought, she'd been invisible to Lydia that other time, and obviously still was.

The nurse and doctor left the room, and Alexander

beckoned to Sabrina to come over as he spoke to his mother.

'They're still waiting for more results before they can give us much idea of the prognosis,' he said quietly. 'But you must go home, Lydia, and get some rest. I'll stay tonight, and for as long as I'm needed.' He glanced across at Sabrina. 'You remember my secretary Sabrina, don't you, Lydia?'

Lydia turned listless eyes to Sabrina. 'Yes—yes, I remember.'

'Well, we'll take over for now. I'll get them to call a cab for you—and try not to worry too much. They tell me that all is not lost.'

Lydia got slowly to her feet, obviously thankful that someone was there to take over, her tears starting again. 'I feel so wretched, Alexander...' she began, and he interrupted.

'Of course you do—you're worn out. And you've had a shock. You must try and hold on, Lydia.'

'No—no, I mean I've not been a good wife to Angus. I know I'm selfish and have always put myself first when I should have thought more of him—and of you two boys, too...'

Alexander held his mother away from him for a second, a look of puzzlement crossing his features. Was this Lydia talking?

'I owe Angus so much—I owe him everything. He was the only one who understood me, understood everything about me,' Lydia whispered.

'What do you mean, Lydia?' Alexander asked quietly.

Lydia let several moments pass before she went on. 'He's the only one who ever knew the truth about me...about my upbringing.' She swallowed, but now for a moment her eyes were dry. 'My parents—your grandparents—didn't die in a car crash as I'd always told you. They gave me up for adoption to a couple who never really wanted children after all. They liked the idea, but not the reality. And a few years later—I was about ten—they divorced. My adoptive mother had to bring me up alone. I learned all about life from her... Oh yes—how to make men notice me, to always put myself first, not to let family get in my way... To stand up for myself because no one else would do it for me.'

Still holding her, Alexander rested his chin on the top of his mother's head as she spoke, unable to believe what he was hearing.

'I was very young when I met Angus, and when he asked me to marry him I couldn't believe my luck,' Lydia went on calmly, as if she was giving a recitation. 'He was everything I was told I should try and catch—a good-looking man with money. But he was so much more than that. He was kind and generous, and he always forgave my failings and promised he would never leave me. And I couldn't bear life without him. We...we understand each other, you see. Although he's away such a lot, he's always there when I need him.'

Lydia stared into space for a moment, as if she was in another world. Then, in a monotone she said, 'If Angus dies, I shall want to die too.' Her eyes filled again. 'I mean it. I couldn't bear the thought of life without him.'

She took a tissue from her pocket and looked up at Alexander.

'And the very best thing he ever did for me was to give me my two wonderful sons—sons I've been proud of all my life. Sons I've never been worthy of,' she added sadly.

* * *

Later that night, as Sabrina lay down on the bed in the private room which Alexander had arranged for her to sleep in, she felt as if she was part of an unfolding television drama. It was so unreal, she thought, so unexpected. By now, she should be at home, unpacking her clothes and reliving her holiday. Instead of that, she'd not only become part of a crisis, she'd seen a different side to Alexander McDonald—a deeply caring side. His love for his sick father was touchingly transparent, and an emerging softness towards his mother was obvious.

After he had seen Lydia safely off in the taxi, he and Sabrina had gone down to the hospital café to have something to eat. Although Sabrina had felt rather embarrassed at being party to everything Lydia had spilled out, Alexander seemed only too anxious to talk about it.

'Today, I think I met my mother for the first time,' he'd said slowly as they drank their coffee. 'She has never spoken of her past before.' He'd paused. 'I have learned one or two things…. It shows that you can't possibly know what makes people who or what they are,' he'd added.

Now, Sabrina pulled the unfamiliar duvet around her shoulders. At least the fact that they'd come straight from the airport meant they had their clothes with them, and that she could clean her teeth and wear a nightdress in bed. Though whether she'd get a wink of sleep was another thing—especially as she would rather have stayed by Angus's bed with Alexander and shared his anxiety. But he had been insistent that she should rest.

'Goodness knows what I might need you for tomorrow,' he'd said as he dropped a light kiss on her cheek. 'Sleep well. I'll wake you if there's any change.' He'd hesitated, pulling her towards him. 'And thank you for coming here with me, Sabrina.'

She'd gestured helplessly. 'If only there was something I could do,' she'd said.

'But you're doing it,' he'd replied softly. 'You're here.'

For the next thirty-six hours it was touch and go with Angus.

When Lydia returned to the hospital on Monday morning, she found Sabrina sitting alone in the ward. As the older woman came in, Sabrina stood up quickly.

'I—I've taken over for a couple of hours, Mrs McDonald,' she explained. 'Alexander is tired out, so I made him go and have a rest.'

Lydia smiled, still looking wan and distressed. 'That is very kind of you, Sabrina,' she said. 'Thank you.'

Well, that was another surprise, Sabrina thought. She'd half-expected to be met with resentment that she, a comparative stranger, was here at all during this sensitive family time. Especially as she was only a secretary.

At that moment a nurse came in and, going over to the bed, she made a little exclamation.

'Ah, Mr McDonald, you're looking a bit better,' she said gently. 'Look—your wife is here to see you. How are you feeling?'

And amazingly, after a few seconds, Angus croaked, 'I'm feeling…f-f-fine. Thank you.'

The next few moments passed in a blur as the doctor was called urgently. As Lydia stood cradling her husband's head, Sabrina slipped away to fetch Alexander.

When she got to the private room, he was standing by the window, his hands in his pockets, and Sabrina went over and touched him gently.

'You're needed, Alexander,' she said. 'I think you should go now.'

He turned quickly. 'My father hasn't…? He's not…?' he said almost savagely, and Sabrina smiled.

'No. He's just told everyone that he's feeling fine.' She paused. 'I'm sure you'd like to hear it too.'

After he'd gone, Sabrina began to finish packing the few things she'd taken from her case, ready to go home.

'Obviously, you must stay at home until I get in touch with you, Sabrina,' Alexander had said when she'd told him she was going. 'I don't know when I'll be back at work—I'll stay here for ever if necessary—but as soon as the situation becomes clearer I'll ring you.'

As she collected her few things from the bathroom and zipped up her wash bag, Sabrina paused for a moment. She had never met Angus McDonald before—not in the proper sense—but she knew she liked him. And she really, really wanted him to get better. For Alexander's sake—and, yes, for Lydia's too.

One evening, ten days later, Sabrina arrived home to find Melly and Sam had also returned. Before they got their greetings underway, the doorbell rang. Immediately Sabrina got to her feet and went to answer it. Alexander stood there, holding a large parcel wrapped in brown paper.

'Alexander!' she exclaimed, not bothering to hide her pleasure in seeing him again. 'What…? Why…? I mean, sorry—come in!'

Alexander grinned down at her and followed her into the house. 'Oh, well, I was just passing,' he said. They both knew he was not 'just passing'. 'And thought it was a good opportunity to drop this off.'

Sabrina didn't know what he was talking about, but they went inside where Melly and Sam were having coffee. Sabrina said brightly, 'You haven't met my sister, have you, Alexander? Um, Melly, this is my…my boss, Alexander McDonald. I don't think I ever actually mentioned his name.'

Alexander put the heavy parcel carefully down against the wall, stood up and went over, holding out his hand.

'Hello, Melly,' he said easily. 'I've heard a great deal about you.'

Melly smiled up at the handsome face, clearly impressed at meeting the famous Alexander McDonald.

'I am so glad that your father is making such a good recovery,' she said, thinking that, if she had to listen to one more word about her sister's employer's troubles, she'd go mad.

'Thank you. Yes, it's an enormous relief all round,' Alexander replied.

Melly glanced down at Sam. 'And this is my partner, Sam Conway,' she said.

The two men shook hands and Sabrina said, 'You'll have some coffee, won't you, Alexander?'

'Thanks—yes,' he said.

Sabrina passed Alexander his coffee. Glancing at Melly, she wondered if her sister was comparing him to the other famous brother she'd met once or twice. Well, there was no comparison, Sabrina thought. Not in looks, style, manner—anything at all.

Alexander stood up. 'Now,' he said. 'I have something to fix upstairs.'

Sabrina stared at him. 'What do you mean?' she said.

'I have a small task to undertake, that's all.' He smiled down at her slowly. 'You can come and help me.'

Together, the pair went out into the hall and Sabrina helped to tear the brown paper from the parcel. When she saw it, she gasped in admiration.

'Alexander! Is this…is this for us? You shouldn't have! It's gorgeous… It's absolutely fantastic!'

'I knew you'd like it,' he said. 'I asked Colette to pack it with tender, loving care.' He lifted the ornate, heavy mirror and began going up the stairs, Sabrina following. 'As soon as I saw it, I could imagine it hanging where the other one had been,' he said over his shoulder. 'My problem was in keeping it a secret from you—but you were far too busy with your own purchases, fortunately.'

It was mid-December before Alexander asked Sabrina to return to work. Now, as she made her way along the familiar street to number thirteen, she felt glad at last to be getting back into a routine. She certainly hadn't wasted the time at home, but being paid to be away from her desk had begun to make her feel useless.

The time alone had got Sabrina to thinking. Seeing how happy Melly and Sam were, and the little ways the two had demonstrated their deep feelings for each other while Sam had been staying with them, Sabrina felt a familiar, small stab of envy. They were so obviously in love, she thought. They could have been made for each other.

While Sabrina was thrilled and happy for them, deep down she recognized another less comfortable feeling: that the umbilical cord between Melly and her had been severed once and for all.

But all this introspection was nothing compared to

how she was feeling about her employer. Her employer. Her boss. Someone who *did* need her. Oh yes, he needed her all right…for now. He'd told her so, several times. She had fulfilled all her secretarial duties to the very best of her ability—staying late or coming in early whenever he'd asked, making him countless coffees and lunches, and one or two suppers too. And she'd gone with him to France, because that was what he'd wanted at the time. She'd allowed him to make love to her because that was also what he'd needed. Then he'd needed her to be a consoling presence in that hospital ward. So what? He was paying her handsomely for all her efforts, wasn't he?

Sabrina slowed her steps for a moment. Be honest, she told herself. He might need her, but she needed him too—because the hard fact was she knew she loved him deeply. She'd fought against it, not wanting to risk a passion that might end in yet more pain. But it was a lost cause. Useless. Because he didn't love her—not in the way that her heart yearned for. And she doubted that Alexander McDonald could ever profess his love for her, or any woman. It was just not in his nature.

Sabrina let herself into the house with her key, then made her way upstairs. It seemed a long time since she'd been here, she thought as she went into the study. So much had happened…

There didn't appear to be anyone else around. Maria had obviously already gone, and there was no sign of Alexander. As she went over to her desk, Sabrina suddenly spotted the large, leather-bound book lying there; immediately knowing what it was, she picked it up eagerly: it was their novel. Its weight in her hands made her realize just how much work had gone into it—not that she needed telling.

Carefully, almost reverentially, she opened the first page of *Symptoms of Betrayal, by Alexander McDonald*. Sabrina's hands almost shook as she looked down at it, a feeling of personal pride entering her consciousness. She had been there while this famous writer had fashioned a lot of this; had watched him covertly as he'd wrestled with the difficult parts; had shared his relief when that final chapter had come together...

As she continued staring at it, Sabrina read the first couple of pages which contained the author's imposing list of previous publications. There were the usual acknowledgements, together with the usual disclaimer about all characters being fictitious, and then... Hardly believing her eyes, she had to sit down for a moment.

On the page immediately preceding chapter one was the dedication—just two words, dead centre, saying simply:

For Sabrina

That was all. Sabrina's first sensation of shock was followed by one of incredulity and choking emotion. There had never been any discussion about a dedication, and seeing her own name there had almost taken her breath away.

She sat back for a moment, her eyes still fixed to the page. Well, of course; that had to be his way of expressing his gratitude, she thought. A little pat on the back for her loyalty—perhaps by now he was running out of friends to include.

Whatever his reason, Sabrina was overcome, and she had to fight back her tears. It was a privilege, and she did feel honoured.

As she reached for a tissue from her bag, a piece of

paper fell out and fluttered to the floor. It was the application form for the new position which Emma had rung her about. Sabrina had kept putting off filling it in, but maybe now was the time. Maybe her duties here had run their natural course and now, with Alexander's novel safely under wraps, she should call it a day. Because she loved being here too much, and was beginning to forget that she was a highly qualified psychologist with another life out there, another world that did not include Alexander McDonald.

In his sitting room two doors along from the study, Alexander sat brooding silently, staring into space. He had heard Sabrina come in but had wanted her to see the book—their book—before they came face to face this morning. He had delayed her return to work until now because he'd needed some time away from her to see whether he could face the future without her. To convince himself, one way or the other, whether she really had become as indispensable to him as he thought. But he knew the answer to that. He'd known it for a long time.

Suddenly, he stood up, strode purposefully along the landing and thrust open the door to the study. This had to be the moment of truth, he told himself. He couldn't bear to wait another day, another hour…

Sabrina looked up and smiled quickly, indicating the novel in front of her.

'Oh, Alexander,' she said. 'Doesn't this look good? Doesn't it look lovely? It's great to see the finished product.' She paused. 'You must be very proud of it.'

He shrugged. 'Well, aren't you?' he asked bluntly. 'I seem to remember there were two of us on the project.'

So, she'd been right, Sabrina thought. He clearly thought he'd pay her the compliment of adding her name.

'And thank you—so much—for the dedication.' She swallowed. 'I could hardly believe it.'

He came over and glanced down at the application form which Sabrina had begun filling out.

'What's that? What are you doing?' he asked frankly.

Well, she supposed he had every right to ask; he was paying her for her time here.

'Oh, this is the application for the post my ex-colleague rang me about when we were in France,' she said casually. 'And don't worry; even if I'm successful—which is by no means certain—the post isn't open until the end of March, so we'll have plenty of time before that to concentrate on your next novel.'

'Don't!' he said harshly. 'Don't do this. I don't want you to go.'

Sabrina's shoulders sagged slightly. She knew that he needed her skills, and it was undeniably true that she seemed to fit in with all his requirements, tick all the necessary boxes. Of course he didn't want her to go. What else had she expected?

But Sabrina knew that she must think more of herself and less of him on this occasion. And as she looked up at the impossibly handsome face, at those eyes which had always seemed able to read her innermost thoughts, she knew she must put a stop to it now. She could no longer bear to be close to him—and not be loved by him.

'I'm sorry, Alexander,' she began. 'But I feel it's right that we should part company soon.'

'Why?' he demanded roughly. 'Why is it right? I

thought we were good together, you and I, Sabrina. We could go on being good together, couldn't we?'

'What exactly do you mean by that?' she asked.

'Well, what I mean is, I want us to be together—properly. To commit to each other.' He shook his head irritably. 'I mean, I want you to marry me, of course! What's the problem?'

For a second, Sabrina felt almost amused at the question; now was the moment. 'You're the problem, Alexander,' she said, surprised at her own coolness of tone.

'Why? Explain!' he demanded.

Looking up at him, her bewitching eyes moist and full of emotion, Sabrina said, 'I agree that we are good together.' Would either of them ever forget their one passionate night together? 'But I don't think you understand me, Alexander. I am more than aware of *your* needs—your wants—but I don't believe that you're aware of mine. You simply have no idea,' she added quietly.

'But, if you leave me, I'll never find out what your needs are, what you're talking about!' He thrust his hand through his hair. 'If it's about wanting to return to your own profession one day, well, of course I fully understand. I'd never stand in your way. You could set up your own consulting room here, if you wanted—there's plenty of space. And you could still go on working for me. We'd sort it between us somehow. But don't leave me, Sabrina. You'll have to give me time… That's all I'm asking for—time…'

'Time is not what you need,' Sabrina said slowly. 'What you lack, Alexander, is the ability to utter the one thing I—or any woman—would expect to hear you say. Well, three things, actually.'

'Which is? Which are?'

After a long moment, staring straight in front of her, Sabrina said slowly, 'I want you to tell me that we should be together, that we should commit to each other, simply because *you love me*—and for no other reason. I want you to force yourself to say it—to say, "I love you".' She swallowed, quietly amazed at her own temerity. She was giving her boss instructions! How had she found the courage to do that? But she was forcing him to give her a reply now. It would be his only chance; she knew that. And after a moment she repeated what she'd said. 'I want you to tell me that you love me, Alexander. Is that such a hard thing for you to do?'

In the complete silence which followed that remark, the two were like solemn players in a momentous production which was about to reach its climax; the intensity in the room was palpable, and painful. Then Alexander walked slowly over to stare out of the window, his hands thrust in his pockets.

'Perhaps I should explain something,' he said. 'About Angelica.' After a few moments he went on. 'I met her at one of my book signings. Or, rather, she was in the long queue of people which the organizers were trying to hurry along.' He paused. 'On these occasions there are always those who want to engage in conversation and chit-chat, and the whole procedure can drag on a bit. This particular day did seem endless because hundreds had turned up.'

Alexander waited before going on. 'Anyway, I'd glanced up once or twice and I'd seen this tall, raven-haired, beautiful girl… Well, you couldn't miss her. She never actually got to where I was signing. But eventually she was the last one, and we exchanged pleasantries as she gave me her book.' He paused. 'She asked for the entry to read "for Angelica"—and "never give up". Which I thought was a bit strange at the time,' he added.

Alexander turned to glance back at Sabrina briefly. 'Then later, as I left the building to go the car park,' he went on, 'there she was. She'd somehow managed to park her car right next to mine—she must have been there very early in the day to do that.' There was another long pause.

'She asked if she could buy me a drink. Well, it'd been a long day, and suddenly the thought of spending an hour in the company of a very attractive woman seemed…enticing. So I bought us some dinner and it was midnight before we parted company. We exchanged phone numbers…you know how you do…and I thought she'd been good company: intelligent, and a good listener. She hung on my every word, and I suppose I had my head turned a bit.' Alexander turned to stare out of the window again. 'Well, this was all a very long time ago,' he added defensively.

'For the next two or three months we saw quite a lot of each other—and I even began to wonder whether she'd be the one I'd marry and settle down with…' A derisive snort left Alexander's lips.

At this point, Sabrina got up and came across to stand next to him, knowing that he wasn't enjoying telling her all this, but he went on.

'One evening, I was invited to go with her to someone's twenty-first birthday party. It was at a wine bar in town, and very crowded. Plenty of bright young things there, a lot of excitable noise and merry-making and plenty of drink to go with it. I knew it wasn't my kind of thing, but anyway…' He shook his head slightly. 'Unfortunately—for both of us—I enjoy very keen hearing. Later in the evening I overheard Angelica talking to two friends.' Alexander grimaced to himself. He could recall the incident without difficulty.

'The long and short of it was that Angelica's purpose in making herself known to me was to get to Bruno. To get to my famous brother. She apparently had great ambitions for herself in the theatrical world—something she'd very skilfully kept from me, by the way. My brother's name had barely been mentioned between us. Up to that point I'd been listening to everything she was saying with only half an ear, but when Bruno's name cropped up I immediately took more interest and it all became clear. Especially when I heard Angelica's final remark.' Alexander's mouth twisted as he remembered.

'"As soon as my feet are fully under their family table, who knows what'll happen for me? Alexander could be my fast track to success at last...perhaps even stardom! And then telesales can take a run and jump!"'

'That's what she said,' Alexander went on flatly. 'It wasn't me she was interested in at all—it was Bruno, who could maybe give her the chance to progress her stage career. And, looking back, I had to give her full marks for her enterprise. She'd made me feel that I was the only man on the planet that she had eyes for.

'But her final words to her friends were, "I'll do whatever it takes... You know me. Persistence is all—and I never, never give up—not when I really, *really* want something".

'Then I remembered what she'd asked me to write on the book, and it left me in no doubt about her true motive in hanging around to speak to me.'

There was complete silence for a few moments as Sabrina took in everything Alexander had told her. How dreadful that must have been, to be used as a tool in someone's ambitions—and especially to get to a close relative. How hurtful and how degrading for him. Being degraded was something Alexander McDonald would not have experienced before, and something he would never tolerate again.

'So our wonderful "relationship" ended that night—and I've never seen her since,' Alexander said noncommittally. 'Neither have I seen Angelica's name in lights either,' he added.

Gently, Sabrina put her arm around Alexander's waist and rested her head on his shoulder. 'I'm sorry that you had to tell me that, Alexander,' she said. 'But I'm glad that you did because it does answer my question. To be treated in that way is unforgivable—well, I wouldn't be able to forgive it if it happened to me,' she said bluntly. 'But I can understand your reluctance to actually tell someone—tell a woman—that you love her...'

At that, a slow smile spread across Alexander's features and almost hungrily he gathered Sabrina up in his arms, virtually crushing her to him.

'Sabrina,' he whispered, his lips lingering over her hair and her neck. 'I have never said those words to anyone because, I suppose... Well, because...' He frowned briefly. 'I have never heard them actually said to me. They are words which have always seemed unreal, belonging to another world, just out of my reach.' He gazed down into her eyes, making Sabrina almost melt with longing and tenderness.

'But since I met you I have found myself whispering those words, Sabrina, whispering them to myself. And now I'm going to say them out loud. For the first time in my life, I'm going to tell someone that I love them. *I love you, Sabrina Gold. I love you.* With all my heart, my soul and mind.'

And as he uttered the words, Alexander felt the

loosening of a lifetime's tension, felt the unbelievable magic of laying his soul bare to someone he knew he would trust and adore for the rest of his days—if only she would have him.

Leaving him in no doubt about that, Sabrina wound her fingers around his neck, drawing him even closer to her. She tilted her head back, offering him her parted lips, all her senses swimming with emotion and happiness. Because she knew that he had unlocked that part of her she'd thought she'd lost for ever. For her, there was to be no more running away.

Today was the beginning of the rest of her life—of their lives.

And she knew it was going to be wonderful.

MODERN

JORDAN ST CLAIRE: DARK AND DANGEROUS
by Carole Mortimer

Helping aristocratic actor Jordan St Claire recuperate from
an accident, physiotherapist Stephanie McKinley discovers
the man behind the famous façade…and he's determined to
unleash her reserved sensuality!

BOUND TO THE GREEK
by Kate Hewitt

Greek tycoon Jace Zervas hires Eleanor Langley—the flame
he extinguished years ago—purely for business. But, secluded
under the hot Mediterranean sun, Jace finds the fire of passion
still burns…

RUTHLESS BOSS, DREAM BABY
by Susan Stephens

Magenta isn't expecting the old-fashioned ruthlessness of her
new boss Gray Quinn! He'll give her the night of her life, but
he might not be there when she wakes up… And he definitely
doesn't want her taking maternity leave!

MISTRESS, MOTHER…WIFE?
by Maggie Cox

Dante Romano has fought hard to get where he is today—but
nothing compares to discovering he's the father of a child.
Marrying Anna Bailey is the only option to right the wrongs of
the past…so he'll see her at the altar, willing or not…

On sale from 7th January 2011
Don't miss out!

*Available at WHSmith, Tesco, ASDA, Eason
and all good bookshops*

www.millsandboon.co.uk

MILLS & BOON®

are proud to present our...

Book of the Month

St Piran's: Penhally's Wedding of the Year & St Piran's: Rescued Pregnant Cinderella

from Mills & Boon®
Medical™ Romance 2-in-1

ST PIRAN'S: THE WEDDING OF THE YEAR
by Caroline Anderson
GP Nick Tremayne and midwife Kate Althorp have an
unfulfilled love that's lasted a lifetime. Now, with their
little boy fighting for his life in St Piran's Hospital…can
they find their way back to one another?

ST PIRAN'S: RESCUING PREGNANT CINDERELLA
by Carol Marinelli
Dr Izzy Bailey is single and pregnant when she meets
the gorgeous neo-natal nurse Diego Ramirez. When
she goes into labour dangerously early Diego is there to
rescue her… Could this be the start of her fairytale?

Available 3rd December

Something to say about our Book of the Month?
Tell us what you think!

millsandboon.co.uk/community
facebook.com/romancehq
twitter.com/millsandboonuk

2 FREE BOOKS
AND A SURPRISE GIFT

We would like to take this opportunity to thank you for reading this Mills & Boon® book by offering you the chance to take TWO more specially selected books from the Modern™ series absolutely FREE! We're also making this offer to introduce you to the benefits of the Mills & Boon® Book Club™—

- **FREE home delivery**
- **FREE gifts and competitions**
- **FREE monthly Newsletter**
- **Exclusive Mills & Boon Book Club offers**
- **Books available before they're in the shops**

Accepting these FREE books and gift places you under no obligation to buy, you may cancel at any time, even after receiving your free books. Simply complete your details below and return the entire page to the address below. You don't even need a stamp!

YES Please send me 2 free Modern books and a surprise gift. I understand that unless you hear from me, I will receive 4 superb new books every month for just £3.30 each, postage and packing free. I am under no obligation to purchase any books and may cancel my subscription at any time. The free books and gift will be mine to keep in any case.

Ms/Mrs/Miss/Mr _____ Initials _____

_____

Surname _____

Address _____

_____

_____ Postcode _____

E-mail _____

Send this whole page to: Mills & Boon Book Club, Free Book Offer, FREEPOST NAT 10298, Richmond, TW9 1BR

Offer valid in UK only and is not available to current Mills & Boon Book Club subscribers to this series. Overseas and Eire please write for details.. We reserve the right to refuse an application and applicants must be aged 18 years or over. Only one application per household. Terms and prices subject to change without notice. Offer expires 28th February 2011. As a result of this application, you may receive offers from Harlequin Mills & Boon and other carefully selected companies. If you would prefer not to share in this opportunity please write to The Data Manager, PO Box 676, Richmond, TW9 1WU.

Mills & Boon® is a registered trademark owned by Harlequin Mills & Boon Limited. Modern™ is being used as a trademark. The Mills & Boon® Book Club™ is being used as a trademark.